THE EYEWALL SEEKER

VICTORIA KIMBLE

WALL CLOUD PRESS

For all those who live in the paths of hurricanes.

Your fortitude and resiliency is the stuff of legends.

Chapter 1

MOM WAS GOING TO notice that I packed two bags. I had
to pack two bags; I couldn't fit everything into one
bag. And then she'd want to know what I had in the
second bag. And then she'd want to know why I had so
much weatherproofing gear. And she'd know I was lying
because she *always* knew when I was lying. It was like her
superpower or something.

Mom entered my room for the twentieth time. "Do you
have a warm enough coat? What's the temperature going
to be while you're there? Do you want to borrow one of
mine?" She laid three jackets on my bed.

I heaved out my best exaggerated sigh. "Mom. Relax.
Seattle is basically Castle Rock, just with more clouds and
rain. This one will be fine." I held up my lined raincoat,
grateful that I didn't have to lie about that. I *was* taking the
raincoat. Just not to Seattle.

She sat on my bed and stared at all the clothes piled
up next to the suitcase. "I know you're only packing for
a week-long trip, but it reminds me that in a few short
months, you'll be packing for college." She blinked fast, a
telltale sign she was trying to keep tears from running
down her face.

"Oh, Mom." I sat beside her and looped my arm through hers. "You always tell me to take one day at a time, right? Don't get ahead of yourself."

She sniffed and laid her head on mine. "I'm sorry. I'm dealing with unresolved grief over your sister and brothers moving out, and this is triggering for me."

I laughed. "Sounds like you've been spending time on Trig's therapy app again."

"It's a good app. You should set up an account. It might help you with all the transitions you have to deal with."

I wanted to pretend like I didn't know what she was talking about. So many giant things were happening all at once. My graduation from high school next month should have been the only thing I had to adjust to, along with my move to Eckman University on the Western Slope of Colorado in August. But Mom meant my break-up with Mason a few weeks ago. She might be right. I hadn't talked to anyone about it. Not her, not Trig, and not even Dasha, my best friend. I couldn't bring myself to tell any of them that the reason we broke up was because Mason said that he didn't want to have to think about me when he entered the Air Force Academy after graduation. It was too humiliating.

She also meant my adjustment to Chip Sinclair being a part of our lives. I had promised her I would give her relationship with Chip a real chance, but the truth was I lied about that, too. I had no plans to give it a real chance. Not until I had actual, solid proof Dad died in Hurricane Goliath.

"Maybe I'll do that after my trip." I hugged her arm. That wasn't a lie. After this mission, I might need to work through some things with a therapist. I may be only eighteen, but even I knew that a journey into a fifty-year-old hurricane would be traumatic.

Mom kissed my hair. "Oh, I just remembered why I came in here. Do you have a bag for laundry? You'll want something to put dirty clothes in, so they don't touch the clean ones in your suitcase."

I shook my head. "I'm not going to get that gross."

She gave me a look. "Ashlyn Grace. Your underwear will be dirty every day. You *are* bringing a change of underwear for every day, aren't you?"

"Mom!"

"Well, I never imagined I had to say it, until just now when you said you didn't think you'd have dirty clothes. I've got a laundry bag for you. I'll be right back."

As soon as she left, I had a flash of brilliance. It was one that set me up for ridicule with my family, but I was willing to pay that price.

"Mom!" I stepped into the hall and yelled. "Where's the Widow Maker?"

"The Widow Maker? Are you allowed to even have something that big?" She poked her head out of her room. "Are you serious?"

I nodded. "It'll be fine. I mean, we all have to check our bags on the bullet train, anyway."

"Hmm. Check the closet in Penn's room. I moved a bunch of stuff in there so it would be easier to get to things."

I flashed her a grin, then headed from our top floor down to the basement. Penn's bedroom was practically a cave down there, but it was perfect for him. It kept his mess away from the rest of the house.

Or, I guess I should say it used to be perfect when he lived here. My stomach squeezed as I stepped into his old room and flipped on the overhead light. The room didn't look like a part of our house. There were no clothes piled on the floor, no crumb covered plates on the empty dresser, and no trash shoved under the bed that didn't even have sheets on it anymore. It still had the faint aroma of dirty socks and corn chips, though. I guess that smell was baked into the carpet.

The closet in that room was the biggest closet in the house. Mella and I used to argue about who should get that closet, but neither one of us wanted to give up our rooms with natural light on the top floor. As a result, Penn's perk of having to live in the basement meant he had a huge space to shove his mess.

Since Penn moved out, though, Mom had already taken over the closet with the things she used most often. Sure enough, our largest suitcase, the Widow Maker, stood within easy reach in that closet.

I grabbed it and hauled it upstairs. It was easy to drag around when empty. As soon as I filled it, it would be much harder. If Trig still lived here, I would make him help me.

The first thing I noticed when I got back to my room was the fabric laundry bag on my bed. Mom was so smart. I did need that. I closed my door, hoping she wouldn't come in and out anymore. I really needed to organize my stuff so it would be easy to get to tomorrow, and I didn't want an audience for that. She would only ask questions I didn't want to answer. And I didn't want to lie to her again.

I had just finished burying the empty duffel bag under a stack of shirts in the Widow Maker when someone knocked on my door and opened it without waiting for me to answer.

"Ash!" Dasha burst in and flopped on top of the unpacked clothes on my bed. "You're not packed yet?"

I put my hands on my hips. "I'm almost done. I mean, I will be, as soon as you get off those clothes."

She grinned and rolled off my bed. "Sorry. I finished this morning, so I thought I'd come help you."

My stomach grew rock hard as I forced a smile. Lying to my mom was one thing. Lying to my best friend was another. I hadn't quite figured out this part yet. How was I supposed to tell her that I wasn't going with her on our senior trip to Seattle? She had been planning things for us on this trip for months. It was a school trip, but we had plenty of space to do what we wanted, and Dasha had every spare minute of ours booked.

"Can you pack my makeup and hair stuff? I haven't done that yet." I handed her the small makeup bag that sat next to my clothes.

She squealed and hopped over to my dresser. "What do you want to take? Everything?"

I bit my lip. "Just mascara and eyeliner. And my pink eyeshadow. I mean, we're not doing anything fancy, right?"

Dasha sorted through the cosmetics scattered across the top of the dresser. "I guess you could go the granola route. But don't you want to step it up a little? Mason is going to be there."

I shrugged and kept my back to her as I put things in my suitcase, putting my real clothes toward the top for easy access. "I don't care what he thinks."

"No, not *for* him. But to show him you're still amazing and he's a total scum face for letting his mom tell him to break up with you."

"I wish his mom had forbidden him from going on the trip."

Dasha laughed. "For real. I'm so surprised she's letting him. Oh wait...is *she* going?"

I whirled around. "Oh my gosh. I don't know. I mean, I don't think so. He never said."

"Could you imagine?" Dasha made a face. "I guess I wouldn't be surprised at all if she came. And not even that Mason wouldn't have said anything about it. I mean, he's so used to her holding his hand through life that it would be so natural. He wouldn't even think to say anything because he truly doesn't understand how weird it would be."

Before Mason and I broke up, I would always steer the topic of our discussions away from Mrs. Woods, out of a twisted sense of loyalty to the woman I always hoped would end up as my mother-in-law. My friends would often joke about her and Mason's relationship, but I never wanted to take part.

Even now, though, this conversation wasn't making me feel better about anything. When I first met Mrs. Woods, I liked her. She was a fun person with a good sense of humor. She only turned controlling once she realized how close Mason and I were. The wedge she drove between Mason and me carved a deep wound that was still so tender that any talk about her or Mason felt like squeezing lemon juice over a paper cut.

"It doesn't matter. Throw in my mascara, eyeliner, that sparkly pink eyeshadow, and my nude lip gloss."

"I'm putting in your eye, cheek, and face palette," Dasha said. "Just in case."

I took a deep breath. "I don't want to think about him anymore. Because I…" I stopped and she whirled around.

"You what?"

"I've, uh, been talking a lot with Luca lately."

Dasha's mouth dropped open. "Luca? The guy from the Storm Chasers?"

I nodded and tried to keep a grin from spreading across my face. "Yeah. He's really, um, cool."

She narrowed her eyes and studied my face. "Define 'a lot.' Like, how often do you talk?"

"We text every day." I looked down at my hands, afraid to look her in the eye. I regretted bringing this up. Luca and I did text every day. Many times throughout the day, in fact. Often, the texts were about nothing. But then there was the mission we were planning. I peeked up at Dasha. She grinned like a fool.

"Ash. This is great."

"It is?"

She tossed my makeup bag into my suitcase and grabbed my shoulders. "Yes! You deserve to be happy. And I deserve to meet him."

I laughed and wiggled out of her grasp. "You will. Soon. I promise."

She flopped back on my bed. "Has your family met him? Is he coming over tonight? I mean, it *is* a goodbye dinner."

"No!" My face heated. "No way. They don't know about him. And there's nothing to tell. We're just texting, okay?"

Dasha sighed. "Fine. But as soon as we get back from Seattle, I'm meeting him. Okay? I should meet him before your family, anyway. That way, if he's amazing, I can put in a good word for him with your fam. And if he's a real troll, then I can snap you out of it before Trig and Penn get to him."

I squeaked out a laugh as the familiar guilt about the Seattle trip wormed its way up my throat. It wasn't too late; I could still go to Seattle. I had already paid for the trip. My seat hadn't been given away. My best friend was expecting it. And it would make my life easier.

But my dad was nowhere near Seattle. The last thing my family heard about him was that he went missing in Hurricane Goliath, somewhere south of Atlanta, as he tried to make his way to the eye ten years ago. And the Storm Chasers had evidence that he stayed in a shelter near Gainesville, Florida, three years ago.

Florida. On the complete opposite side of the country from Seattle. I had to go to Florida. I tucked my lightweight shirt deeper under the heavier shirts meant for Seattle so no one would see.

"Yes, for sure. You'll meet him soon." I smiled at Dasha and stuffed the guilt down deep. I had made my choice.

CHAPTER 2

My door burst open and hit the wall. Dasha and I shrieked, and I grabbed the nearest object I could find to fight off the intruder. I was aware that a stuffed bear might not be the best choice, but I would make do.

Trig pointed at us and doubled over with laughter. "You two should see yourselves. You look hilarious, huddled together. Ash, do you think that bear is going to protect you?"

I growled, jumped off the bed, and pounded him over the head with the bear. "You jerk! You can't bust into people's rooms like that. And this is what the bear can do!"

"Ow, stop! You're hitting me with his hard nose."

"Good!"

He grabbed the bear and tried to wrestle it away from me. He was stronger than I was, but I had learned a few tricks as the youngest of four kids. I twisted around and dug my fingers into the bear's fur. Perfecting the Death Grip is Youngest Kid 101 stuff.

Dasha was on the bed, clutching her stomach as she laughed at us. "Guys, stop. I'm going to pee my pants."

I gave one more tug and yanked the bear out of Trig's hand. "Dash, this isn't funny."

"Yes, it is. Trig, that was hilarious."

He puffed out his chest and smoothed back the hair that had fallen out of place during our struggle. "Thank you. It was some of my best work."

I scowled. "So it's okay when Trig breaks in, but not when Julian does it at your house."

"Exactly." Dasha's grin was cheeky. "It's an older sibling thing. Julian hasn't earned the right, because he's just a dumb baby brother."

I rolled my eyes and turned back to Trig. "When did you get here?"

He made himself at home on my desk chair. "Two minutes ago. I snuck in and up here before Mella roped me into whatever she's doing."

Mella had taken over our kitchen earlier that day to make my goodbye dinner. As the oldest of us four kids, she had had plenty of practice cooking actual meals since she had taken care of so much while Mom worked. She had only moved out three weeks ago, but Mom and I already missed having home-cooked dinners. Mom rarely got home until late, and I wasn't good at cooking, so I stuck to pod meals and anything that only required the flash cooker.

"She's making lasagna from scratch. She came over here this morning to start the sauce." I tossed the bear at Trig and turned back to my suitcase. It was almost ready.

"Whoa, the Widow Maker? Are you moving to Seattle?"

Dasha threw another bear at him. "She *needs* all that stuff. We can't go to Seattle and look like tourists. We need to fit in."

Trig narrowed his eyes. "How long is the trip again?"

My chest grew tight. I had no idea how long I'd be gone. The senior class would come back from Seattle in one week.

There was no way this mission would be over by then. "Uh, just a week. But I had to pack two different outfits for each day, because I don't know if it's going to be cold and rainy, or nice and sunny."

"And the weather app can't tell you?"

"It says a chance of rain every day, but you know that even now they can't predict the exact timing of the rain this far out."

"Yeah, Trig. Tech has come a long way, but Hurricane Goliath taught us we still can't be sure what the weather is going to do." Dasha clapped a hand over her mouth and looked at me with wide eyes.

I gave a small smile. "It's okay, Dash. You can mention Hurricane Goliath."

Trig nodded. "Yeah, we don't freak out when we hear that name. I mean, we can't go a day without hearing it from somewhere. We've made peace with it."

Trig and the rest of my family may have accepted the United States Hurricane Agency's position that my dad had been lost in the storm, but I hadn't. Dasha was the only one who knew that I had raided USHA with the Storm Chasers last month to get the tech we needed to go on the next mission.

The reason Dasha was afraid to mention Hurricane Goliath was because she thought I was still upset about missing out on going into the storm with the Storm Chasers. Because that mission was happening at the same time as the Seattle trip.

"Anyway, Trig, any chance you could stay here tonight and help me get my suitcase to the light rail station in the morning?" I batted my eyes and pushed out my lips.

He groaned. "Ugh, fine. But all I can do is get it to the station. How are you going to manage that beast after that? You'll need to get it on the light rail, then to baggage checking at Union Station, then to your cabin in Seattle."

I shrugged. "There will be boys around. Jude or Zed will help."

"They didn't stick with Team Mason?"

Dasha reached over, grabbed the bear she had already thrown at Trig, then leaned back and threw it at him again. "Mason doesn't get his own 'team' because he's a jerk. Besides, we don't need boys. I can help. Or Gretchen. She's crazy strong."

Trig studied my face. "Are you going to be okay with him there?"

I pushed away the lump that tried to grow in my throat. "Yeah, I'll be fine. There will be plenty of space for me to avoid him. And Dasha's right; Gretchen *is* crazy strong. So, will you help me tomorrow or not?"

Trig nodded. "Of course. Besides, I haven't seen Mason since before, you know. I want to go make him uncomfortable."

Dasha and I laughed. Good ol' Trig. Besides lying to my mom and my best friend, one of my biggest regrets about my entire plan was not telling Trig. I wished he could come with me. But it was too big of a risk. No one could know what the Storm Chasers and I were about to do.

"Hey, I need help down here!" Mella called up the stairs. "If you want to eat sometime today, come help me!"

Trig stood up and saluted. "We've been summoned." He ducked out the door, then thundered down the stairs, making as much noise as possible.

Dasha grinned. "I love your family."

"It's a good night when they're all here," I said. "Can you stay for dinner? Or are you having a goodbye dinner at your house?"

"I can stay. We had a goodbye lunch because Julian has a baseball game tonight."

I looped my arm through Dasha's and we marched down the stairs together. This was going to be the greatest night. I loved when all of my siblings came home for dinner. It had only happened twice in the last three weeks. When they all broke the news that they were moving out, they said that we would have a weekly family night, but so far that hadn't worked out. No one could agree on a consistent day of the week that would work with their schedules and social calendars. Mom said it might take time for it all to sync up, but I was starting to think that weekly dinners were just a dream that would never happen.

I needed everyone I loved close tonight. I wasn't sure when I'd see them all again. Or if I would. No, *when* I would. The mission was going to be a success. I was going to make it to the eye, I was going to find Dad, and I was going to bring him home so that Chip would go away.

"Hey, it's Ash and Dash!"

Dasha and I froze in the doorway. Chip stood in my kitchen. With an apron on. Holding a pan of garlic bread. I glared at him, but he shot me a look that said, *remember our agreement? You keep your yap shut, and I make sure nothing bad happens to your family.*

Dasha let out a high-pitched giggle that she only used when she was nervous. "Oh, um, hi Mr. Sinclair." She clutched my arm tighter.

I schooled my features. "Hey, Chip." That's all I could manage, though. I didn't plan to ask him how he was doing.

Chip grinned. "Dasha, you may call me Chip. Ashlyn does, and you're practically sisters."

Dasha shook her head. "No way. My parents taught me to respect adults by calling them by Mr. or Mrs."

"Ah, yes. Livvy told me all about the Harts. I love their old-school morality. I can't wait to meet them someday."

I swallowed the anger that was on the verge of spewing out of my mouth. There was no way I wanted Chip to ever meet the Harts. They were too important to me. And I didn't need one more family in danger of Chip's mobster connections.

"Chip, that needs to go in the oven right now."

I wanted to hug Mella. Maybe her bossiness would be the one to drive Chip away. I loved that she didn't care who he was; she was going to tell him what to do no matter what.

"Oops, sorry." Chip gave a sheepish smile, then put the pan in the oven. Mom came into the kitchen with a cake box in her hand. Penn was hot on her heels, trying to reach around her to open the cake box.

Mom swatted his hand. "Gross, go wash that hand. Do you even wash at the shop?"

Penn sniffed his hands. "What's wrong with them?"

"Back in the old days, guys who worked on cars had oil-stained hands," Chip said as he folded his arms and leaned against the counter. "But cars these days still use *some* fluids, right?" Mella glared at Chip. I was shocked when he caught the hint and moved out of the way.

Mom chuckled. "Chip, if you want to still help, you can get glasses of water for everyone. Penn, go wash whatever fluids you have off of your hands. Ash and Dash, can you put forks around the table? Trig should be done putting around the extra chairs."

Dasha and I grabbed the utensils and made a beeline for the dining room. Trig was sitting in a chair, resting his feet on the table.

"Gross, Trig."

"Don't worry. This is where Chip sits."

I grinned. "Excellent. Maybe you'd feel better if you took your socks off and rubbed your toes right there."

Dasha shot me a look. "I had no idea he was going to be here."

"Oh, for sure. He's a part of the family now." I focused on putting the forks around the table. When I got to Chip's spot, I dropped his fork on the floor. Twice. I wiped it on the back of my pants and set it at his place.

"Real mature, Ashlyn," Trig said.

I stuck my tongue out at him and turned to Dasha. "Don't worry. To his credit, Chip usually blends into the background during our family dinners. I've come to appreciate when he can keep his mouth shut." She giggled as everyone from the kitchen came pouring into the dining room with a full lasagna dinner to be set on the table.

Dinner went as I had hoped. Chip quietly ate his food while the rest of us chattered on like we always had before he intruded. Trig and Penn had just finished telling the story of how their downstairs neighbor set off their fire alarm every single morning while making toast when Chip cleared his throat and tapped his knife on his glass.

Mella gave him a side-eyed glance. "What is this, a toast?"

Penn cracked up. "Don't burn it like Dave in 2C!"

Chip grinned and reached for Mom's hand. My heart pounded. If they announced an engagement, I was going to freak out.

"Not a toast, but I have something I need to share with the family." Chip gripped Mom's hand tighter as she eyed him with a confused expression. He looked at me. "Today I formally submitted my bid for candidacy for President of the United States."

I held his gaze and kept my lips clamped together. So, he was going through with it. I had hoped that he was just blowing smoke when he told me on my driveway the day he threatened my family and the Storm Chasers.

Everything was silent for several seconds until Penn let out a muffled burp. Mom glared at him, then turned back to Chip. "I thought you weren't going to say anything yet."

Chip let go of Mom's hand and put his arm across the back of her chair. "Since this dinner is about celebrating Ashlyn's trip, I thought I'd toss my good news in too."

Mella twisted her napkin. "Wow, president, huh? That's, uh, intense."

"Yeah, it is. I mean, it will be. But I wanted to tell you, because this doesn't affect just me. It affects all of you." Chip glanced around the table, then looked back at me. "You all are a part of this. I'll do my best to keep the eyes off of you, but since we're practically family, you are inevitably going to have some of the spotlight shed on you."

I decided to lose the staring contest Chip had started, and I looked at Mom. "What do you think about this?"

She tucked her hair behind her ear and gave a smile. "It's a big deal, but I'm on board. I mean, I support Chip. He's done wonders as director of USHA. Our country could use that organization."

I leaned forward. "Yeah, but what do you think about our family being involved?"

"Well, I don't think it will affect you kids too much. You all have your own lives away from here. We'll bring you to the big things, but the day-to-day stuff will mostly revolve around Chip. Even I should be able to do my work quietly."

"Don't worry, Ash," Chip said, as he leaned back in his chair. "I'm very good at protecting those who are close to me. It's those who aren't under my protection who should have to worry."

The lasagna in my stomach threatened to come up. Why was Chip telling me all this now? How many times does he have to threaten me and my family? Did he know about the mission?

I picked up my water glass and held it up. "Here's to Chip and his candidacy."

He gave me a grin of victory, then picked up his glass and clinked it with mine. "Thanks for your support, Ashlyn. I mean it."

The rest of my family erupted with questions about Chip's campaign while I focused on finishing the rest of my dinner. All my inner turmoil about whether I should go to Seattle or Florida vanished. I was going to Florida. There was only one thing that could get us out from under Chip's thumb, and that was finding Dad.

CHAPTER 3

"Trig, you sound like you're about to poop your pants. Or give birth to a baby." I glanced around the crowded platform of the light rail station. People stared at him as he gave loud grunts that echoed off the metal overhangs. Not strangers either, but my classmates and their families. I hated that my face must be a beacon of embarrassment.

"Did you pack Penn in here? Penn? Are you okay? Can you breathe?" He made a huge show of knocking on my suitcase and putting his ear to the side.

I rolled my eyes and reached for the handle. "Okay, this is far enough. Thank you. I really only needed you to get it out of the trunk. I can roll it from here."

Mom tugged on Trig's coat. "It's time to let go, Little Dude."

He let go of the handle and shook out his arm. "Mommy. My arm feels like a wet noodle."

I pushed him away. Why had I decided that it was a good idea for him to come? "Okay, Drama King. Thank you for your service. I'll bring you back a present."

His eyes brightened. "Ooo, like some Pacific Northwest salmon?"

"No, like a com cover."

Mom laughed at his frown. "Okay, well, I guess this is it. Do you have everything? Do you have a backup com charger? How about lip balm?"

A wave of uncertainty washed over me. I hadn't considered what this moment would be like. Mom was asking questions like this was a normal trip, and for the thousandth time, I wavered. "Yes, I have what I need. The charger, the lip balm, everything." Also, the pair of waterproof boots she hadn't seen.

"Ash!" The shriek of my name came two seconds before Gretchen crashed into me.

Trig grabbed my arm before I fell over. "Whoa. You've got some power there."

She blushed. "Oh, um, thanks."

Did she have a crush on my brother? How had I never seen that before?

"Dasha said you can carry this four thousand pound suitcase because you were crazy strong. Is it true?" Trig pushed the Widow Maker toward her.

Gretchen's face turned a deeper shade of red, but she squared her shoulders and stuck her chin up. Classic Gretchen bravado. "I am crazy strong." She grabbed the handle and lifted the suitcase six inches off the ground for a few seconds before dropping it back onto the platform.

Trig's eyes lit up. "Impressive."

Dasha and Rosalie bounced into our group, snapping Trig and Gretchen out of the flirt bubble they had created. For a minute, I couldn't wait to fill Dasha and Rosalie in and grill Gretchen on the train. But then I remembered I wasn't going with them.

Dasha looped her arms through mine and Gretchen's. "Let's move this way."

Rosalie grabbed my suitcase handle. "Yeah, like, now."

"Why?"

Dasha leaned in. "Because Mason and his mom just showed up, and you guys are blocking the entrance to the platform."

I widened my eyes. "Oh, wow, thanks. Um, let me say goodbye to my mom."

Rosalie grunted. "Whoa, what's in this suitcase? Bricks?"

Gretchen grinned. "I've got it." She grabbed the handle and rolled it toward an open spot away from the path of Mrs. Woods.

I smiled at Dasha. "I'll be right over."

She shot a scowl over my shoulder before heading over to stand with Rosalie and Gretchen.

I turned to Mom and Trig. Mason stood about twenty feet away. Before I could even react, I had made eye contact with him. Sorrow and hurt filled his eyes. Anger washed over me. How dare he act hurt? He was the one who told me he didn't want to have to think about me anymore.

"Do you want me to punch him?" Trig's voice was low next to my ear.

I turned my back to Mason and laughed a little. "No. It's okay. No more energy on him. Not brain energy, not physical energy."

Mom pulled me into a hug. "Good girl. You're doing great. One day at a time."

I wrapped my arms around her and held on tight. My mom was the best support system. My throat closed as I thought about how she might feel later tonight. In about four hours, she was going to realize that I wasn't in Seattle. And she would not know where I was.

Was I being fair to her? She had already gone through so much when Dad went missing. And I was about to do it again. On purpose.

But this was dangerous. I had to keep it a secret. And Chip made it very clear that he would not hesitate to take out me or my family if I messed with whatever he had planned. The less she knew, the better. Plausible deniability.

I squeezed her tighter and buried my face in her shoulder. I didn't want to let go. Everything would change the minute I let go.

Mom laughed and kissed my hair. "Sweetie, you're going to be fine. This trip is exactly what you need to help clear your head. Also, you've earned it. It's your senior trip. A reward for making it through high school."

I nodded and held on for a few more seconds. "Yeah. I just love you. I mean it, Mom. I love you so much. You're the best mom."

Trig snorted. "Sheesh. You're laying it on thick, Ash. You're already the favorite because you're the baby, so ease up."

I grabbed him in a hug. "I love you too, Trig. You're the best brother. Don't tell Penn."

He ruffled my hair before pushing me back. "Uh, I am absolutely telling Penn. Every day."

I laughed as tears filled my eyes. I wiped them away and smiled at them. This was going to work. I was going to find Dad, and then they'd understand. "Okay, well, bye."

Mom kissed my head one more time. "You don't have to check in every day, but text a few times, okay?"

My stomach twisted. "Um, yeah. But, like, don't worry if I don't, okay?"

She rolled her eyes. "Once or twice won't kill you."

Trig grabbed Mom's arm. "Let's go, Ma. I'll text you a few times a day. Will that help?"

I tried to cover up my sadness with a laugh as they walked into the parking lot. I waved one more time as they got in their car. I took a deep breath, then headed toward my friends. Gretchen, Rosalie, and Dasha had their heads close together, and it looked like they were whisper-fighting.

"What's the fight?" I asked, stepping close to the group. Rosalie had guilt written all over her face, while Gretchen and Dasha looked like they were about to punch someone.

"Do you want me to tell her?" Gretchen asked Rosalie. "Because I will. And I won't be nice about it."

Rosalie looked at her with pleading eyes, then turned to me. "I want to sit with Zed on the light rail. Not even the bullet train to Seattle. Just the light rail to Union Station."

Gretchen folded her arms and scowled. "Let me translate: she's going to join Team Mason and sit with them. Because Zed has been stuck to him like glue since you and Mason broke up."

Rosalie threw her hands in the air. "I'm not joining Team Mason! I just want to sit with Zed, and sometimes you have to make sacrifices. He's not going to win me to Mason's side. Mason is a total buttface."

"I still don't understand why Zed can't come sit with us. Why is he acting like Ashlyn did Mason dirty? Did Mason not tell him what happened?" Dasha asked.

My stomach clenched, but only for a second. Letting go of this whole thing with Mason was taking practice, but I was getting the hang of it. Hopefully soon I'd be able to hear his name without feeling like I was getting punched in the gut. The truth was, this was perfect. This was the opening I needed to occupy my friends with other things so I could slip away unnoticed. My actual plans were not something I planned to discuss with the Fab Four.

I grabbed Rosalie in a hug and pressed my cheek against hers. "Rosie, it's okay. For real. I know where your loyalties lie. And I'm okay with you and Zed. Yes, go sit with him." That was one friend down.

Gretchen growled. "I don't like it."

I looped my arm through hers. "You go sit with them too, Gretch, and glare at Mason the whole time."

Her eyes lit up. "Ooo, yes. I'd love to make him squirm. I'll make him think I plan to sit with them the whole way to Seattle. I'll tell him it will give him plenty of time to go over in detail how he lost his mind when he chose the Air Force Academy over you."

I grinned. "Yes, girl. Make him regret coming on this trip."

Gretchen stuck her fist in the air, then trotted over to Team Mason.

"You're okay with this?" Dasha asked.

I grabbed Dasha's arm and pulled her over to the entrance to the station. "Yeah. Um, there's something I need to tell you."

She looked at me with wide eyes. "Are you not over Mason?"

I shook my head. "It's not that. It's just, oh gosh, this is really hard." I couldn't seem to force the words out of my mouth.

She clutched my arms. "Okay, you're scaring me."

I took a deep breath. "I'm not going to Seattle."

Dasha stared at me for a full five seconds, then burst out laughing. "Whatever, Ash. Who cares that Mason is going? Maybe he'll fall into the Puget Sound."

"This is not about Mason. I'm serious. I'm not going."

She stopped laughing and took a step closer to me. "What are you talking about? I don't understand. I mean, you're here. And your mom dropped you off with your suitcase."

"I'm going with the Storm Chasers."

Her face clouded over. "Is this about Luca? Are you trying to get back at Mason by going with Luca?"

I groaned. "No. Of course not. This is about my dad. It's always about Dad. The Storm Chasers have found a path through Goliath to the eye, and I'm going to find my dad."

Dasha shook her head. "I can't believe this."

"It's true. You remember the raid? We got the tech we needed to find the path through the storm. It's high powered radar that shows the accurate picture of Goliath, and Goliath is weak right now. It's only a category three for the next two weeks."

"No, I mean I can't believe you're abandoning *me*."

My mouth dropped. "I'm not!"

"Yes, you are. This is our senior trip, Ash. Our one chance to do something cool before we graduate, and you're stealing it from me."

I was at a loss. "Dash, listen. The storm only weakens like this every ten years. If I don't go now, I'll have to wait another ten years. I can't live for ten more years without knowing the truth about my dad."

She folded her arms. "And what if you don't find him? Then this will all be a waste."

"No, then I'll know I did everything I could. Whatever I find, it'll bring closure."

We stood in an awkward silence for a few minutes. Dasha stared at her shoes, and I looked around the station, trying to give her the space she needed to process. But I had one more thing to ask.

"I need a favor," I said.

"What?"

"Will you take my com with you to Seattle?"

She narrowed her eyes. "Why would I do that?"

"Because I need my family to think that I went on the senior trip."

"Are you kidding me?" Her voice grew loud, and I tried to motion for her to keep her voice down. "You want me to lie for you? And you want to go on this stupid, dangerous trip without a way for anyone to find you?"

"Please, Dash. It's so important. As soon as I get back, I'll be able to tell you everything, but it's for the safety of my family that they think I'm in Seattle."

"So what happens when we get back, and you're still who knows where?"

I bit my lip and shrugged. "I mean, that will happen. But I can't worry about that now."

Dasha shook her head. "What happened to you? Do you know what this will do to your family when they realize they don't know where you are? This will kill your mom. You understand that, right?"

My throat squeezed tight. "Yes. But I have to do this. It's the only way to stop Mom from marrying Chip. And it has to be a secret, or my family could be in danger. Yes, they'll probably hate me, but only for a little while."

"See, that's the part that's missing. Why do you keep saying your family is in danger? Seriously, what kind of danger?"

I twisted my mouth and tried to think of something I could tell her, but nothing came to mind. "I can't say right now. Please, Dash? Please take my com?"

The light rail train arrived at the station, and a cheer rose from all the students on the platform.

"Hey." Luca approached at the entrance. Dasha took a step back, a look of confusion on her face.

"Dasha, this is Luca. Luca, Dasha."

Luca stuck his hand out. "Hey. I've heard a lot about you."

Dasha stared at him, not taking his hand. "I've heard less about you."

I turned back to her. "Please, Dash."

She looked back and forth between me and Luca. "No. I will not lie for you. I'll keep your secret for as long as I can, but I won't pretend like you're in Seattle with me. You'll have to figure out what to tell your mom yourself."

Tears filled my eyes. "Oh. Okay. I mean, I can respect that. Um, have fun in Seattle, okay? I want to hear all about it."

"Yeah, if you make it back. Bye, Ash." Dasha turned and walked toward my classmates, who were all boarding the light rail. I stepped back behind Luca, so no one would see that was I standing there. No one seemed to notice my lone suitcase still on the platform.

"You okay?" Luca asked.

The train left the station with a soft rush of wind.

"No. But there's no turning back now."

CHAPTER 4

THE SILENCE OF THE platform was shocking after the cacophony created by a couple hundred excited high school seniors. I jumped when Luca touched my arm.

"Sorry," I said. "I'm ready." Luca reached for the handle of my suitcase, and I put my hand out to stop him. "Oh, wait."

I pulled out my com and typed before Mom noticed my location.

> Hey, I'm turning off my com now. School rules or whatever. They want us "in the moment to experience the journey."

My heart pounded. How long should I wait for her to respond? What if she didn't? I was about to hit the power button when the three reply dots appear.

> Smart teachers. Text me when you get there! Love you!

My throat tightened.

> Love you too.

I powered down the com as a sob squeaked out. I buried my face in my hands as the wave of grief rolled over me. What had I done?

Luca pulled me into a hug, and I clung to his jacket as the tears poured down my cheeks. I lost track of how long I stood there crying, but I couldn't move until it was all out. I finally took a step back and wiped my nose with the sleeve of my coat. It was gross, but I didn't have anything else.

"Sorry."

"Don't be. I get it."

I glanced at him. "Do you? Have you ever gone on a mission that you might not survive without telling your parents where you were going?"

Luca's eyes softened. "No, I guess not. Unless you count our little side quest into the Disaster Zone last month."

I let out a burst of laughter. "Side quest? Are you a gamer?"

He shrugged. "Aren't we all? Now, can we go?" He grabbed my suitcase one more time, then grunted. "Dang, what do you have in here?"

I rolled my eyes and took the handle from him. "I had to pack for both Seattle and the mission. Since my mom was helping me, she had to see all the Seattle stuff. I'll leave what I don't need at the storage unit. I can do that, right?"

He shrugged, and we headed into the parking lot, me pulling the Widow Maker behind me. His car was an old compact model, and the Widow Maker barely fit in the trunk.

I played with the powered-down com as Luca drove to the storage facility. The black screen seemed to be the perfect representation of the feeling in my stomach. I should have been bursting with anticipation or excitement about the adventure I had waiting for me, but I felt empty.

Had I burned a bridge with my family? Or worse, with Dasha?

I let out a shuddering breath as another tear leaked out. I had thought Dasha would support me. I had been so dumb and self-centered. Of course she was mad that I wasn't on this trip with her. She had been so excited about it. And now I couldn't even do anything to make it up to her.

Luca put his hand on my knee. "Ash. If you want, I can take you home. You don't have to do this."

I wiped my face. "No, I do. I just didn't know how hard it would be to lie to my family. Or how hard it would be to have Dasha so mad at me. I think that's worse."

Luca's hand was still on my knee. I stared at it. Mason used to put his hand on my leg when we drove places. I always loved that. I would lace my fingers through his, and he would pretend like he was driving with one hand, when really the autopilot was in control.

Luca caught me staring at his hand, and he snatched it away. "I'm sorry."

I gave him a small smile. "Don't be. I didn't mind. It was nice."

He put both hands on the wheel and stared out the windshield. "I won't take advantage of you. You broke up with Mason a few weeks ago. It's too soon."

Heat flooded my cheeks as anger flashed in my gut. I did not need another guy making decisions for me. "I mean, I guess. But don't I get a say in this?"

"I just want you to be thinking clearly, and not regret anything."

I shifted and folded my arms. "Listen, buddy. You put your hand on my leg. I didn't do that. And I'm allowed to say that I thought it was nice without you telling me that's not really how I feel. That was the whole problem with Mason, anyway. He seemed to think that he got to decide how I would feel and when."

Luca tightened his grip on the wheel. "Ash, I'm not trying to tell you how to feel. I'm just saying it's okay to be slow about things. Let's just focus on the mission, okay? It's going to take every ounce of focus."

I rolled my eyes and stared out my window for the rest of the drive. I hated he was probably right. Did anything real ever come out of rebound relationships? Did I want something real with Luca? If I did, then he was right; it was too soon. If I didn't, then it wasn't fair to him. Because he obviously was thinking things through. That he had already put so much thought into this turned the burning embarrassment and anger into a soothing warm fuzzy.

Luca pulled into the storage facility and parked in a spot that wouldn't draw attention to the fact that a car was going to sit there for days. He powered down the car and gave me a sideways glance. "We good, Booker?"

I gave a small smile. "Yeah." A rush of adrenaline filled my veins. "Let's go find my dad. Preferably *without* any comments about my suitcase, got it?"

He let out a laugh. "Hey, I get at least three more, since I have to wrestle it out of the car."

I rolled my eyes. "Come on, weakling. I'll help."

To his credit, Luca only grunted twice as we got the Widow Maker out of the trunk and into the storage building. I dragged it to the Storm Chasers unit, and was relieved that most of the team hadn't arrived yet.

Miri Day and Jack Farmer, the two other teens in the group, were there to hold up the rolling door to the unit for us. "Whoa, Denzio. You bringing your whole RV on this mission?" Miri asked.

"Ha ha. It's not mine." Luca shoved her as we walked past, and she nearly fell over.

"Give me a second, guys. You'll be proud." I rolled the suitcase to the corner and unzipped the monstrosity. All of my mission gear was at the top and fit in a pack that would go on my back. I pealed off the layers I had on for Colorado, and put on my lightweight, weatherproof jacket. I shoved the cute fuzzy boots into the suitcase and put on the waterproof boots I had bought without Mom knowing.

I only had a tiny twinge of guilt as I pushed aside the makeup bag Dasha had packed for me. I would deal with that later. I tucked my com in next to the makeup bag and zipped the suitcase closed. As a final touch, I twisted my hair on top of my head and secured it with an elastic.

I turned back around to find Jack, Miri, and Luca all watching me.

"You done getting ready, Adventure Barbie?" Luca asked.

Miri slugged him in the arm. "Shut up. Look, she only has a backpack. I'm so proud."

I grinned. "Thanks, Miri."

Voices echoed in the hall as the rest of the team filed into the unit. Ginger Alpin and Hugh York dragged in large chests on wheels, while Tyler Denzio and Silas Chapman followed behind, each with two big duffel bags.

"Luca. Jack. Go get the other chests." Tyler didn't even glance at his son while he barked the order.

Miri stepped forward. "Why them? You think the girls can't carry stuff?"

"Not everything is a commentary on gender politics, Day," Ginger said. "There will be plenty of grunt work for all of us. For now, I need your help to sort out the rations, and I don't trust the guys to do it."

"Sounds like gender politics to me," Miri scoffed. But she went right over to Ginger's box and flung open the lid. I felt awkward and superfluous for a few seconds; no one had assigned me a job. Then I decided that this was ridiculous. I could help without being asked.

I joined Miri as she pulled boxes of pouch meals out of the chest. They looked similar to the pod meals that Mom and I had gotten used to eating every night, since neither one of us cooked liked Mella. Only these were a third of the size and didn't need to be cooked at all.

"Is this really spaghetti with meat sauce?" I asked, flipping over the package.

"Sure is. Just squirt it right into your mouth and chew," Hugh said. "It's not complicated."

I wrinkled my nose. "But is it good?"

"Everything is good if you're hungry enough. And you'll be hungry, because this is all we have to eat."

"It doesn't look like enough food."

"It's designed to expand in your stomach, Booker." Tyler butted in, a huff in his voice. "And since all the restaurants where we're going were blown away decades ago, this is all you've got."

I scowled. Every word out of that guy's mouth irritated me. He made everything sound like an insult. How was I supposed to know these things? "I wasn't expecting gourmet catering. I've just never seen these before. I'm allowed to ask questions, aren't I?"

Tyler's perma-frown deepened. "We won't have time to hold your hand during this entire mission. You're going to have to pick things up faster."

I clenched my fists. "Since this is the first time I've seen this, and then you told me about it, and then I learned it without having it told to me a second time, I think I pick things up as fast as anyone could. I mean, unless you're expecting me to know things before I've been taught, and then I can promise that you're going to be disappointed."

We stared at each other for five full seconds before I realized that Luca and Jack were back with the other chests, and that everyone was watching us like we were putting on a show.

Silas stepped in between Tyler and me. "We need to go over the plan, but do we need to have a little team counseling first?"

I shook my head. "No, I'm good."

"Yeah, I'm fine too," Tyler said.

Silas studied both of our faces. "I hope you're not lying. Because we don't have any time or room for weird team dynamics. We need one hundred percent trust so that we can move forward. Can you two put aside whatever you have going on so we can do that?"

I nodded, afraid that I was going to get cut from the team. I had to go on this mission. It was the one chance I had to find Dad, and I had already made too many sacrifices to be told that I couldn't go.

I stuck my hand out to Tyler. "I'm cool. I'm good. I won't hold you back, I promise."

He grudgingly shook my hand. "I guess you get the benefit of the doubt."

I sighed in relief as everyone took seats in the folding chairs still set in the semi-circle from the last meeting I had been to here.

Silas remained standing. "Once we get to Nashville, we're going to take the two armored vehicles that our contacts have left for us. They refurbished humvees the military has used to navigate the storm, but these vehicles are about fifteen years old."

I leaned forward. "How are these different? I mean, how do we know they won't get blown off the road?" I remembered too late that I wasn't supposed to be slowing the group down by asking about stuff. I clapped a hand over my mouth and gave everyone an apologetic shrug. "Oops. Sorry. No questions."

Silas grinned. "Questions are fine, Booker. These are low and wide, with aerodynamic panels that shift to allow the wind to go over the vehicles rather than pushing against them. They kind of look like turtles."

Jack groaned. "Please tell me they aren't as slow as turtles."

"We'll be going slow. Low and slow. We have to, to survive those winds. Our plan is to get to the Storm Chasers headquarters tonight, pack up the Turtles, then drive four hundred miles to Tifton, Georgia tomorrow. Tifton is the first base on the edge of Goliath." Silas used his com to cast a map on the wall of the storage unit and traced the path with a laser pointer. "It'll be a long day of driving. The Turtles will only top out at about forty-five miles per hour in good weather, so plan on the whole day."

"You're getting ahead of things, Silas," Ginger said. "First, we have to get to Nashville. We've received intel from our contacts inside USHA that they've upped security on people approaching the Disaster Zone. That means they're watching Nashville."

"Why did they increase security?" Miri asked.

A rock formed in my stomach, and I glanced at Luca. Luca barely shook his head and kept his eyes on Silas. This was my fault. If I hadn't lost my cool with Chip a few weeks ago, I wouldn't have let it slip that the Storm Chasers were the ones to break into his office. Chip was smart; he would know that something was being planned. He promised to forget about the break in if I didn't say anything to Mom, but that didn't mean he wouldn't plan ahead.

"Probably from our raid. We knew they'd figure out we took the tech pads. Don't worry, we expected this," Ginger said.

"We're going to break into three groups and take different routes to Nashville." Silas pulled up another map. "One group will take the direct train from Union Station. One group will head to Omaha, then down from the north. One group will head to Dallas and approach from the southern route."

"Which means we need to divide up the equipment, so if something happens to one group, we won't be crippled, and the mission can move forward," Ginger said.

The rock in my stomach turned to ice. "What could happen?"

Luca glanced at me. "Delays. Don't worry. I'll go with you."

"I'll go with Luca and Ashlyn," Miri said. There was something in her voice that made me pause, and I tried to read her face.

Tyler cleared his throat. "No, I'll go with Luca and Ashlyn. No need to have three teens travelling to Nashville together." I cringed. I would rather travel with Luca and Miri.

"I'll go with Jack and Miri," Ginger said. "We'll take the Dallas route. There's something I want to pick up in Dallas."

"I'll go the Omaha route with Hugh," Sybil said. "I want to drop my kids off at my aunt's. My husband works too much right now to watch them."

Hugh nodded. "Sounds good."

"I'll go with Hugh and Sybil, and we'll pick up the Turtles," Silas said. "Everyone leave your coms here. We'll get new devices at headquarters. And remember, the Turtles leave for Tifton tomorrow at five o'clock in the morning. With or without you."

CHAPTER 5

"Why did he have to come with us again?" I hissed as soon as Tyler headed for the bathroom on the train.

Luca scowled. "To keep an eye on me."

This ride to Nashville had been far less pleasant than the first one I took with Luca. We couldn't talk the way I wanted to, not with Tyler sitting so close. I hoped to ask Luca why Miri seemed so weird about travelling with us. But then again, he probably didn't know. Dudes never picked up on the subtleties of responses from girls.

"He doesn't trust me, and I have no idea why," I said. "He's been like this since the day I met him."

Luca shrugged and shifted. "Once this guy came to a meeting, and he seemed really interested and on board. He came to meetings for months and even helped with some missions. Then this big expose came out in the news about the Storm Chasers. Every word was false, but it turned out the guy had been an undercover journalist. Our funding tanked for a while, and we were stuck until people started coming back to the meetings. Dad has been slow to trust anyone ever since."

My mouth dropped open. "Okay, but that's not my deal. I'm trying to find my dad. What does he think that I'm trying to hide?"

Luca shrugged and cleared his throat as Tyler sat back in his seat.

"Now's the time to rest, Rookie. Sleep when you can," Tyler said. Luca gave me a shrug, leaned back, and closed his eyes.

One silent hour later, we pulled into the Nashville train station. The last time we had come, the station was almost deserted, since people rarely traveled so close to the Disaster Zone anymore. The weather around Nashville had become very unstable over the past twenty years, so most people migrated away from the path of the destructive thunderstorms. They had no idea that the tornados in the Disaster Zone seemed to be under someone's control.

This time, though, the station bustled with activity.

Tyler swore under his breath. "That's military."

Luca sat up and peered out the window. "What are they doing here?"

"I don't know. But let's not get off at the same time. I'll go first and get the bags from baggage claim. Ashlyn, you go next, but wait three minutes. Luca, go to the bathroom now, wait five minutes, then get off the train. I don't even want them to see us sitting together right now."

My heart pounded. I had never been scared of the military before. In fact, because of my mom's work at USHA, and how tightly they collaborated with the military, I had always taken comfort anytime they were around.

But the military and the Storm Chasers were not friends. Any time the Storm Chasers hosted a rally in Washington, D.C., the military had been close by and quick to intervene at the slightest sign of any heightened emotion. Silas said that their actions were borderline excessive, spraying the

Storm Chasers with pepper spray if someone so much as coughed too loud. I always figured he was exaggerating. Now the sight of so many guys in fatigues with guns made me not so sure.

Tyler grabbed his pack and moved to the front of the train, then sat as the conductor made the disembarking announcements. Luca stood and moved to the bathroom, leaving me to sit alone.

I hated feeling so young and inexperienced. What was I supposed to do while I waited? I didn't even have my com to keep me busy. I was glad Tyler wasn't watching me. Everyone else in the Storm Chasers would have known how to make themselves look occupied or not suspicious.

I bent over and unzipped my pack. I dug around, as if I were trying to find something or rearrange the contents inside. That would be a good reason to hang back. I wasn't ready to get off.

Tyler got off the train, and I panicked for a minute. I didn't have a watch to tell me when three minutes had passed. I focused on my feet and started counting, trying to keep the numbers slow and even. As soon as I reached one hundred and eighty, I stood, stretched, and grabbed my pack.

The train attendant had a frightened look on her face as I passed her on the way out the door. Or did she? I took a deep breath to slow my paranoia. This was getting out of hand. There was nothing to worry about. I stepped onto the platform.

"Stop." Two soldiers blocked my path. Each carried a rifle.

I clutched my pack and tried to smile. "Yes?"

"Come with us."

"Why?"

The men paused and leveled their looks at me, as if no one had asked them that question.

"Because we said to."

I hiked my pack up on back. "Are you allowed to just command anyone to come with you?"

The taller of the two men made a show of tightening his grip on his rifle. "Yes, we are. Because if you don't, we can have you arrested for obstructing justice."

"I'm being arrested?"

The shorter man gave a smile. "No, but we need you to come with us. We're asking everyone. See?" He pointed to other soldiers who intercepted the few people as they came off of the train.

I saw through what they were doing. Good cop, bad cop. "But why are you asking everyone to come with you?"

The taller man sighed. "Miss, please come with us so we can get this over with. This is the last train of the day, and the sooner you comply, the sooner we can all get on with our lives, okay?"

Short Man laughed. "He's hungry. We didn't get lunch. And our last job is getting you into a room for questioning."

I sighed in frustration. "Questioned about what? How long is this going to take?"

"Move. Now."

I glanced around the platform, hoping to see Luca, or even Tyler. But they were no where. I swallowed and moved forward, with Short Man leading the way and Tall Man right behind me.

They took me to a room with two chairs and a small table, and not much else. A screen on the wall displayed the time and weather, but that was it. I sat in one chair with my pack on my lap. Tall Man and Short Man left the room and closed the door.

The minutes ticked by. This was not good. Would Tyler and Luca wait for me? Or would they leave me and go to headquarters? I had experience getting left behind. Mason left me at the very first Storm Chasers meeting we had ever gone to. But that was in my hometown. I knew where to go and how to get there. If Tyler and Luca left, I'm not sure I'd remember how to get to the Storm Chasers headquarters. And I had no way of contacting them. I had been relying on being with the Denzios.

I vacillated between fear and anger the longer I waited. My throat felt tight because I had no idea what to do next. The smartest option would be to go home. By now, Mom would realize I hadn't gone to Seattle. She expected my "I'm here and safe" text hours ago. She would be freaking out. I could answer whatever questions they had and tell them I needed to get back to Denver.

I was livid that Tyler withheld so much information from me. How could I be a good team player if I still didn't have a way of contacting anyone? This was ridiculous. He treated me like dead weight, but I was only dead weight because he was keeping me down. I suppose I was just hitching a ride with the Storm Chasers into the storm, but I could take care of myself. I wouldn't be a burden to them if I had all the information I needed.

I jumped up as the door opened. My train of thought had worked me into a fighting spirit, and I was ready to take on whatever they had.

A man and a woman in khakis and polos entered. I almost laughed out loud. They looked like camp counselors I had seen on this funny video series Rosalie liked to watch. I stood by my chair. They looked around the room, a bit confused. I think they expected a third chair.

The man slipped out of the room, and the woman turned to me. "Hi, I'm Detective Shannon. My partner is Detective Curry, and he'll be right back. He's looking for another chair."

"Shannon? Is that your first or last name?" I folded my arms and slumped in my seat. I felt ashamed. My parents raised me better than this. I had never talked to an adult this way. Well, an adult besides Tyler. But Tyler deserved it.

Detective Shannon smiled. "It's my last name. My first name is Sofia. What's yours?"

I clamped my mouth shut as Detective Curry banged into the room with another chair. He tried to put it in the corner, but the table stood in the way. It took him a few tries to wiggle the chair into place, and then he sat down and looked at his partner.

"You good?" she asked him. He nodded. She turned back to me. "So you were just about to tell us your name."

There was no way I was giving them my real name. Mom would have called the police by now, and my name would be all over any runaway teen database. But I had to give them something.

"I'm Lyla." When I was a kid, I hated my name, and begged Mom to change my name from Ashlyn Grace to Lyla Rosepetal.

"Hi Lyla. What brings you to Nashville?"

"Am I not allowed to be here?"

Dectective Curry cleared his throat. "Why are you answering a question with a question?"

I shrugged. "I just don't know what I'm doing in this room. I haven't done anything wrong. I paid for my ticket to come. And now my friends don't know where I am, and my mom made me promise to stay with my friends the whole time."

"Who are your friends, Sweetie?" Detective Shannon leaned forward. "What are their names?"

I sighed. "I don't think I'm allowed to say. I mean, they're very private. Why are you asking me these things? I'm just on a trip before I graduate high school, and my friends and I love music and heard there was still a music museum around here. Like, from before the music hub moved to Grand Rapids, away from the storm."

Detective Curry grinned. "You like country music?"

I smiled back. "Oh yeah. But only the real old stuff, like Shania Twain and Blake Shelton."

He whistled. "Yeah, that's old. You should hit the Bluebird Cafe. They've still got tons of old pictures on their walls. The paper kind, not digital. They're all signed by those old stars, too."

I stood up. "Cool, thanks for the tip! Well, gotta go."

Detective Shannon stood and blocked the door. "Sorry, Sweetie, but we're not done here."

The "sweetie" bit was getting on my nerves. "But why?"

"Let her go, Shannon. She's not with them."

I opened my eyes wide. "With who?"

"The Storm Chasers."

"Detective Curry." Detective Shannon's voice carried a note of warning.

"Come on, she's just a kid on a trip to see old music nostalgia."

"Who are the Storm Chasers?" I asked, trying to keep their attention on task.

"They're this group that's been fighting the government for years about Hurricane Goliath, as if the storm is the government's fault." Detective Curry rolled his eyes.

I laughed. "That's hilarious."

"Yeah. But they've gotten dangerous. They've destroyed government property and have made threats against the cities closest to the Disaster Zone, so we have to watch for them."

"Detective Curry, may I speak with you outside?" Detective Shannon had her mouth pressed in a firm line as she opened the door, and the two left, shutting the door behind them.

Heat burned in my gut. This was Chip's doing. And it was a total lie. The Storm Chasers had never made threats. And I guess breaking the lock on Chip's office door could be considered "destroying government property," but that was a real stretch.

I couldn't focus on his lies right now. The fact was, he was on the lookout for the Storm Chasers. And he was smart enough to start have people looking for *me* soon. I needed to get out of there and warn Luca and Tyler.

The detectives came back in, Detective Curry looking like a whipped dog.

I sat up straight. "I promise I'm not with any storm chasers. I just wanted to see some places where the old country stars used to hang out. But if I see any, how do I let you know? Because I don't want them to ruin any of our history."

Detective Shannon sighed. "You can notify any of the local police stations, Sweetie."

I smiled. "So, can I go meet my friends? They're probably freaking out right now. We said we'd meet at the light rail station if we got separated, and I bet they've been waiting a long time."

"Yeah, go have fun. Be safe."

Detective Curry smiled at me on my way out, and I made myself walk calmly. I had no idea where to find Luca and Tyler. I headed toward the entrance of the train station and tried to think. If I couldn't find them, I was going to need a new plan.

CHAPTER 6

A GUST OF WIND almost knocked me over the second I stepped out of the train station. Dark clouds roiled above me. The weather in Nashville was unstable, and it was evident we had come on a bad day. It's as if Hurricane Goliath knew we were coming for it, and it sent out a warning blast this far north to stay away.

That probably wasn't far from the truth. We still didn't know how, but we were convinced that someone created tornados on command. Luca, Miri, and I had seen the tornados drop from the sky on schedule with our own eyes. It made sense that if someone was controlling tornadoes, they could make thunderstorms, too.

I twisted my long hair into a knot on top of my head, braced myself against the wind, and tried to form a plan. The Storm Chasers headquarters were south, somewhere on the main highway. Luca and I had taken a car last time. I might be able to hitch a ride with someone heading that way. Penn liked to tell stories about how people hitchhiked in the old days. Of course, most of his stories were about escaped convicts from the prison system.

I headed toward the light rail station across the train station parking lot. The screen there would have a map, and I needed to get my bearings.

A clap of thunder boomed out as someone grabbed my shoulder, and I screamed and swung around.

"Whoa, Booker! Watch that right hook." Luca had his hands up to protect his face from my fist.

I punched him in the arm. "If you don't want a black eye, then don't grab girls from behind."

"Ow. Gosh, you hit hard."

"I have two brothers. They taught me well."

He pulled me into a hug. "I thought you were a goner."

My heart quickened, and I wrapped my arms around his middle, tipping my head back to meet his eyes. "So did I. I thought I was going to get arrested, or worse, that they were going to call my mom."

His gaze dropped to my lips, and for a brief second, he looked like he might kiss me. Butterflies fluttered to life in my stomach. What about all the things he said about not taking advantage of me, and how I had just broken up with Mason? And did I even want him to kiss me?

He broke the hug and trotted backward. "Come on. Dad is waiting for us a few blocks away."

I hurried beside him and raised my voice to shout over the wind. "Where did you go? Did you get stopped?"

"I saw them grab you, so I waited in the bathroom for a while. Then I got off with the crew, and hid behind them. They didn't question the crew."

I rolled my eyes. "I wish I had thought of that."

"Don't worry. Your spy brain will kick in soon enough. I'm sure you'll be better at sneaking around than I am."

We ducked inside a fast food Mexican restaurant that didn't look like it got very many customers. Tyler sat at a table with his back to the wall, facing the door. The grumpy scowl on his face actually brought me comfort. I needed familiar right now.

"Where have you been?" he growled.

I plopped my pack down on the ground and sat down hard in the chair. "Oh, buying souvenirs and getting my nails done."

Tyler leaned forward. "We don't have time for games."

Luca sat in the chair between us. "Dad, we're doing fine on time. We even have time for tacos. Then you can ask all the questions you want."

"Tacos will take too long."

"No, they won't. And we'll take a bunch to the farm. Come on; this will be the last chance for a good meal for who knows how long."

Tyler twisted his mouth and headed to the counter to order.

My mouth dropped open. "How did you do that? I mean, get him to change his plan?"

Luca grinned and tipped back in his chair. "Tacos are Dad's weakness."

Tyler came back with two bulging bags of tacos, and we each grabbed two. They weren't great. But I savored them anyway. Luca's words about this being our last meal once again reminded me how dangerous this mission was. I hated to admit it, but Tyler was right. We weren't playing a game.

"Talk," Tyler said around a mouthful of taco.

I sighed. "They made me wait in a room. Two detectives came in and asked for my name."

"Did you tell them?"

"Are you going to interrupt every single time I take a breath?"

Luca leaned in between us. "Guys, there is no time for fighting. Dad, let her talk. She's going to tell us everything, right?"

I heaved out a sigh. "Of course I am. I did not tell them my real name. I told them my name was Lyla, and that I came to Nashville with some friends to see a country music museum."

Luca stared with his mouth open. "And they bought that?"

I tossed my hair over my shoulder. "You know, it's good I'm so young. A teen coming to Nashville on a star searching trip is a believable cover story."

Tyler took a bite of taco and studied me. As soon as he finished chewing, he grunted. "Yeah, I guess you're right."

"Anyway, the man detective gave me some great tips on where to find old country music nostalgia. Then he told his partner that I wasn't with 'them.' She seemed annoyed that he let that slip."

"Who did they think you were with?"

"The Storm Chasers."

Tyler and Luca exchanged an uneasy glance.

"Why did they ask about the Storm Chasers?"

I crumpled my taco wrapper. "Because I think Chip tipped them off. They said that they are on alert in all major cities on the edge of the Disaster Zone, because the Storm Chasers threatened violence against the cities."

Luca slammed a fist on the table. "But that's not true. The Storm Chasers have *never* been violent. Or even threatened violence."

Tyler didn't seem surprised. "Of course not. But the threat of violence would be a reason to send the military to guard entry points."

I grabbed one more taco. "Before we go to headquarters, we need to stop at a store. I need hair dye. And scissors. If Chip has already sent the military, then it won't be long before he puts out an alert on me."

Tyler narrowed his eyes. "Why on you?"

"Because he's dating my mom. And by now, Mom knows that I'm not with my class in Seattle. And that I turned off my com, and she'll be freaking out because she doesn't know where I am." My voice caught. I still hated the idea of what she would be going through. And I hated myself for doing this to her on purpose.

Luca put his hand on my arm. "That's smart. If Chip can activate the military, he can put all law enforcement on alert for Ashlyn."

I wiped my nose and squared my shoulders. "I wouldn't be surprised if Chip tells everyone that the Storm Chasers kidnapped me."

Tyler pursed his lips. "Okay. We gotta go. We can't be in town for much longer."

I put my unwrapped taco back in the bag, sad that I didn't get to eat it right then. But he was right. We needed to go. "That drugstore across the street will have hair dye."

Luca stood. "I'll go. Ashlyn, you go wait in the car. Dad parked it down the street. Dad, give her the tacos and come with me."

I put my pack on my back and Tyler handed me the two bags of tacos. "Keep your head down. Don't talk to anyone, not even if they knock on a window. We won't be long."

I swallowed hard and nodded, and we split up. The wait in the car felt like it took hours, even though only ten minutes passed. I was terrified of someone causing a scene and letting Chip know where I was.

I shouldn't have worried. The streets of Nashville were abandoned, especially with the strong winds blowing. Lightning flashed overhead. It was obvious the natives knew when to hunker down. Tyler and Luca got into the car, and Luca handed me the supplies.

I flipped over the box of hair dye. Luca had chosen a sunny golden color that looked great on people with blue eyes. My eyes were hazel. I wrinkled my nose. "Blonde?"

He shrugged. "I thought it looked the most natural. The last thing we need is you with purple or pink hair, drawing attention."

We arrived at the Storm Chasers headquarters in Murfreesboro just as it was getting dark. The storm clouds made the evening light darker earlier than it should have been. Jack and Miri flew out the door of the farm house as soon as we came to a stop.

"You're late." Miri folded her arms across her chest and frowned.

Luca got out of the car and held up the bags of tacos. "But we brought food."

Jack pumped his fist in the air and took the bags from Luca. "Man, we thought you guys weren't coming."

A crack of thunder rattled the surrounding buildings, and we all grabbed the packs and bags and hurried into the farm house.

Ginger sat at the table studying several tech pads, each one with a different image. She glanced up. "Denzio, thank goodness. We gotta rethink travelling without communication."

Tyler set his things down and crossed to her command center. "Yeah, that wasn't the smartest thing we've done."

I was shocked. Tyler admitted that he did something wrong? I wanted to call him out, but Luca was right; we couldn't keep fighting. And I knew I bugged Tyler as much as he bugged me. We had to figure out how to build some trust.

"So what happened to you?" Miri had plopped herself at the table with four tacos in front of her.

"The military took over the train station. Didn't you see them?" Ginger, Miri, and Jack would have arrived at the train station an hour before us.

"We saw them. But Miri pretended to be about to puke, and Ginger said she was so worried about her that the guys let her through to the bathroom," Jack said.

"And Jack looks like he's ten years old, so they assumed he was my baby brother." Miri grinned.

"Well, I got stopped. They're looking for Storm Chasers. Chip told them that the Storm Chasers are going to blow up cities near the Disaster Zone."

Jack's eyes bugged out. "Whoa, seriously?"

"That's messed up." Miri scowled as she unwrapped her taco. She kept her eyes narrowed as she looked at me. "But where was Luca?"

Luca sat in the seat next to her. "I didn't get interrogated. Then we stopped for tacos, and we came here."

Miri glanced from Luca to me, a look of doubt on her face. My stomach twisted. I liked Miri, but I felt like maybe she didn't like me as much. The wound from my fight with

Dasha hadn't healed, and the thought of Miri upset with me was like pouring salt on it. I really needed an ally on this trip.

I tried to smile and offered to get Miri a drink to go with her tacos. That's when I noticed her hair. It was the same shade of blonde that Luca had picked out for me. Did he do that subconsciously? Did he have feelings for her, and he was trying to make me look like her?

There was nothing I could do about that now. I grabbed the hair dye and scissors. "I have to go cut and dye my hair, in case Chip has put out a missing teen alert on me."

Miri and Jack kept eating their tacos, as if people changing their appearance was a normal occurrence during a Storm Chasers mission. Luca gave me a chin up nod and reached for a taco himself.

It took me a few minutes to work up the courage to cut my hair. I loved my long, light brown hair. It had been that way since junior high. Mason had loved it, too. I fingered the ends as I stared at myself in the mirror, but reminded myself that it was just hair. I could re-color it, and grow it out again. I rushed through the hair process, cutting my hair to the top of my shoulders. I couldn't bring myself to cut off any more, and I wanted the option to put my hair up. Still, it was a full hour before I finished the dye process. I didn't have time to dry my hair to see what it looked like, but that didn't matter anymore. I twisted the wet hair into two small buns at the base of my head and rejoined everyone on the main floor.

Miri and Jack were trying on jumpsuits that were designed for the rain and looked way sturdier than the jacket I brought. Miri glanced at my hair, then handed me a jumpsuit.

"We can't wait. The window closes soon. Tomorrow, by my calculations," Ginger was saying.

Tyler rubbed the back of his neck. "They have the vehicles. We can't go into the storm without them."

"What's going on?" I asked Luca as I sat next to him on the couch.

He did a double take when he saw my wet hair. "Whoa."

I glared at him. "You picked the color."

"Hugh, Silas, and Sybil haven't shown up yet," Miri said. "They have the Turtles."

A knot formed in my stomach. "And we can't contact them because no one brought coms."

Tyler scowled. "I already said that was a mistake."

I held my hands up. "I'm not accusing. I'm just listing out the facts."

My eyes filled with tears. Was the mission already a bust? We had to go. I couldn't go home at this point. I had already broken my family's trust, hurt my best friend, and dyed my hair. There had to be another way.

Luca reached over and grabbed my hand. "Don't panic, Booker. We just have to pivot."

"How?

The door to the farm house banged open, and we all jumped. Even Tyler. Silas stood in the doorway, dripping wet. "Whoa. Sorry, did I scare you?"

Tyler jumped up. "We didn't hear you drive up. We were just talking about how to go on without you."

Silas gave a wry grin. "Good man. Mission first. You won't hear the Turtles. They convert wind energy to fuel the vehicles, so their engines aren't any louder than the wind is at any point."

Jack got up and ran to the window. "Whoa, those look sick!" Each Turtle was the size of a school bus, but they were much wider and lower to the ground. They resembled pictures of old Ferraris, only much longer. The wheels were huge and thick, designed to drive the vehicle up and over things.

"Uh, won't these be a problem if we run into flooding?" I asked.

Silas grinned and shook his head. "These Turtles are part duck. We can drive through water, as long as it doesn't cover the top. We just have to readjust the panels to move on top of the vehicle, and it'll pull us through."

Sybil wrestled with the giant door of the shed where they kept the planes, and Hugh waited to drive inside.

We all filed outside into the wind to help load the Turtles with the supplies in the shed. Storm Chasers had been leaving communication and survival equipment in the sheds for weeks. At first, it seemed impossible that we were going to get all the supplies and ourselves in, but the guys packed them like puzzles. Each Turtle could seat six people in the front part of the vehicle, and then the rest of the Turtle was open for storage.

It took until midnight to finish packing the Turtles. Every time I thought we were done, Tyler would point to another crate filled with communication tech, extra batteries, camping equipment, or food. My muscles shook every time I tried to lift something, and my ears hurt from the sound of the wind hitting the metal shed. The loud roar did not let up, and we had been shouting at each other all night.

We filed back into the farm house, and Ginger headed to the command station to pack up the tech pads. "Okay, get some sleep. We leave at four a.m."

CHAPTER 7

NOBODY WARNED ME ABOUT the time paradox inside the Disaster Zone. Every hour felt like it lasted a day, and at the same time, I panicked that the seconds moved so quickly while we did not.

I bit back a groan as Silas radioed our vehicle that we needed to stop for the tenth time. I'm not exaggerating; we had stopped nine times already.

"Let's go," Tyler barked. I tightened the hood of my rain jacket around my face. I suppose I should have been thankful that at least it wasn't raining. Or that we hadn't seen any tornados dropping out of the sky yet. But the wind was brutal.

I slid open the door of the Turtle, once again marveling at the ingenuity of these vehicles. They really had been designed to drive into hurricane-force winds. All the doors slid open and stayed close to the vehicle, so there was no chance of the wind catching the door and snapping it off. They had put handles along the inside of the door to help get ourselves out into stormy conditions, or to grab to help get ourselves back into the Turtle. We clipped long metal ropes to harnesses built into the rain jumpsuits Ginger had gotten in Dallas. They let us go about fifty feet away from the Turtle, and were strong enough to catch anyone who got tossed by the wind. The wind wasn't strong enough to push us yet, but Tyler and Silas made us clip in every time, so we'd get used to the process. The further we got into Goliath, the more necessary it would be.

The trip from Murfreesboro to Atlanta had gone pretty smoothly. Slow, because the Turtles' maximum speed was only about forty-five miles per hour. But the way was clear, and we reached Atlanta in about five hours, which had given me a false hope that the road to the eye was going to be easy. I figured the only danger we had to focus on was someone trying to stop us from reaching the eye. I spent that whole part of the trip worrying about Chip and what blockades he had used USHA's resources on.

I should have been more worried about Goliath. The further we got into the Disaster Zone, the harder the wind blew. The dark clouds churned overhead, suggesting a constant threat of torrential downpour. And the darkness was otherworldly. The time on our watches showed early afternoon, yet the sky gave the impression that we were moments away from needing nighttime shelter.

Once we got past Atlanta, we had to stop every ten miles or so to move debris off the road. It had taken us four hours to go sixty miles. No one had to tell me what to do anymore. Tyler, Hugh, Silas, and Luca hauled the largest logs and branches out of the way, and the rest of us scanned the road for anything small and sharp that might get kicked up into the gears of the Turtles. We didn't need damaged vehicles on top of everything else. We had a few tools and repair supplies, but anything major would cripple us.

This stop was one of the easiest. It only took us five minutes to clear the path. But the stops were getting more frequent, thanks to the fact that the harnesses only allowed us to clear a fifty-foot radius.

We tumbled back into the Turtle, and Luca slammed the door shut. Miri handed out water bottles, and we all took a minute to catch our breath. Tyler picked up the radio to let Silas know we were ready to move on when a gust of wind blew a branch over the top of the Turtle, making a loud scratching noise.

I stared out the window, unsure of how long I could keep the fear from taking over and causing a complete breakdown. "Um, how much farther to Tifton?"

Tyler grunted. "Would you check the tech pad?"

I hadn't expected him to ask me for help. I dug the pad out of the box behind my seat and fired up the GPS. My heart sank, but I put on my cheeriest face. "Only one hundred and twenty-one more miles to go. Let's see, at forty-five miles per hour, that will take us—"

"Two and a half hours," Miri broke in. "But we're not going forty-five, are we?"

A grim look had replaced Tyler's perma-scowl. That scared me more than the dark clouds. "No. We've only gone about twenty-five since Atlanta. The Turtles can go over a lot of debris, but not very fast."

"And that doesn't include any stops we're going to make to get the big stuff," I said. I swallowed hard. "Well, we have to keep moving forward, right? I mean, we're not going back, are we?"

Another large gust slammed the Turtle, rocking the huge vehicle. Tyler swore and punched a few buttons to readjust the wind panels. The wind was getting worse. I stared out the window. There wasn't much to see. The wind had ravaged most trees, and there were no buildings along this stretch of road. I was amazed at how silly I had been. If this was what the Disaster Zone looked like, then what was Goliath going to be like? I kicked myself for letting my naïve mind believe that Dad could have gotten through this. I wasn't sure we were even going to survive getting to Tifton; how could anyone survive going into Goliath?

A tense silence filled the Turtle, and then Tyler pressed down the button on the radio. "Silas, we need to make a decision about our plans. Over."

"Copy. Hang tight. I'll come to you."

Silas jumped out of his Turtle and ran against the wind to ours. He did not clip on his harness, and for a minute I wondered if he would get blown away. Miri moved back to make space for Silas to jump in. He slid open the door, jumped in, and slid the door shut almost in one fluid motion.

Tyler turned around in the driver's seat. "We're still one hundred miles away from our destination. Can we make it?"

Silas glanced around. "There's a shelter in Macon. We should head there and regroup."

I quickly typed on the tech pad. "That's twenty-four miles. We can make that."

"Macon? We never talked about Macon," Tyler said.

Silas shrugged. "That's because I thought we could make it to Tifton. But let's go, before it rains. Ginger said we're on borrowed time; the rain is going to start any second, which will slow us down even more. And we need to be in some kind of shelter before nightfall."

He pulled open the door without waiting for any agreement from Tyler and exited the Turtle the same way he got in. I held my breath as he pushed against the wind, only relaxing when he made it in the driver's seat of his Turtle.

"Well. Good thing we've got a stop in Macon," Miri said.

Tyler powered up the Turtle and tightened his hands on the wheel. "Yeah, good thing. You know what I always say about good things, Luca."

Luca looked uneasy. "Good things are too good to be true."

This was new. I was used to bearing the brunt of Tyler's distrust. I was not used to him casting a shadow of doubt on anyone else. Especially not Silas.

We crawled forward, only having to stop two more times to clear the road before we reached Macon. Seeing battered, abandoned cities was still a new experience for me. They were so creepy. Most buildings looked like the citizens had tried to fortify them, probably in the first few years of Goliath. But then USHA declared this area part of the Diaster Zone, and had forced the people to move north.

The radio crackled to life as we crossed into the city limits. "The shelter is on the other side of town," Silas said. "But we may have to clear the roads a few more times."

"Copy." Tyler rolled his head from side to side, trying to loosen his shoulders. He had been more tight-lipped than usual since Silas mentioned the shelter, and it was clear that the day had taken a toll on him. Even though it still felt early and like we could make a few more miles, I was glad we were stopping for the day. If our team was too tired, then we would be at risk of making fatal mistakes.

The rain started just as we entered town. It wasn't a gentle start, either. First there was no rain, then there was a deluge coming at us sideways, as if we were being sandblasted with knives. The windshield wiper on the passenger side snapped off in seconds, and Tyler swore under his breath.

We made it through town without stopping, but we had to slow our already snail-like pace to a crawl. I wasn't sure how Tyler and Silas were able to maneuver the Turtles around the debris in the narrow roads of town in the blinding rain. These roads were not built for vehicles as long as ours.

"Is that it?" Miri asked as she tried to see over Tyler's shoulder through the clear part of the windshield.

"It looks like it. I mean, it looks like the specs I've seen of the shelters in the storm. I just didn't know there was one here," Tyler answered.

Silas' Turtle headed toward a large, windowless structure that looked out of place in a field. As we got close, I could see that the entire building was made of concrete. A carport made of concrete stood on one side of the structure. The carport was wide enough for the Turtles to drive right in, and long enough to fit all of Silas' and half of ours. At least we could exit our doors under the shelter. The wind and rain were pelting the side of the carport and not coming in through the open sections.

Silas hopped out of his Turtle and walked right up to a door. He pressed his palm on the pad outside the door, and the door swung open.

The team poured inside the pitch black room.

"Hmm. The lights aren't working," Silas said from somewhere to my left. "Jack, get the lanterns."

We huddled near the door until Jack got back with three battery-powered lights. Silas switched them on, and we got a full look at the inside of the building.

Enough bunks for sixteen people lined two of the walls. The wall with the door had a stove that looked like it was a hundred years old. One corner had a curtained off area.

Silas grinned and pointed at the curtain. "That's the bathroom." Jack ran over and pulled open the curtain to reveal a toilet that looked like the toilets found in state parks. The kind you don't flush. I groaned. The curtain didn't provide near enough privacy.

Jack's cheeks turned red, and he looked at his shoes. "Uh, I'll be the first to use this, if you don't mind."

Ginger pulled a small device out of her pack and switched it on, a white noise filling the room. She set it on the floor close to the bathroom area. "There. Do your thing. Let's all agree to just not look at or listen too closely to what goes on behind the curtain, okay?"

Everyone chuckled and nodded, the absurdity of the bathroom situation helping to relieve some of the tension of the day.

Then Tyler ramped back up the tension. "So, why wasn't this shelter part of our planning?" He folded his arms and scowled at Silas.

Silas looked surprised at being the target of Tyler's scowl. "I told you. I thought we'd make it to Tifton tonight."

"But how did you know about this one? Do you have the locations of more shelters than we do?"

Silas sighed. "I guess I do. Matteo gave me the locations of about a dozen shelters like this one. I wasn't keeping them a secret. I just thought you'd only care about the ones that applied to us."

Hugh stepped in between Silas and Tyler. "Does it matter, dude? I'm just glad we didn't have to push on through to Tifton, and risk driving in the dark."

Ginger nodded. "There's no way we would have made it. And our radar can tell us where the rain is, but it can't help us navigate. I think we should be grateful."

I shivered and wrapped my arms around myself while the adults argued about whether we should be happy about the shelter. I thought of the heavier coat that I had left in the storage unit in Colorado. Maybe I didn't pack right. I knew it would be wetter here, but I didn't expect it to feel so cold.

Luca stepped up beside me and wrapped his arm around my shoulder. "You okay, Booker?"

Warmth curled in my belly, and I snuggled in closer. "Yeah, just cold. And glad we're stopping for the night. I had no idea the weather would be this bad."

He grinned. "Uh, did you know the mission was in a hurricane? The weather is bad in a hurricane."

I bit back a smile and bumped him with my shoulder. "Duh. There's just a big difference between knowing in your brain and experiencing it."

He nodded and rubbed my arm to warm it up. I caught Miri watching us through narrowed eyes, and shame filled my chest. I really needed to find out if there was something between Luca and Miri. I didn't want to come between them, or steal anyone from Miri. But Luca had a choice in the matter too, didn't he?

"Sorry guys, there's no wood for the stove," Sybil announced. "Body heat only tonight."

"That's our *own* body heat in our own beds," Tyler growled, looking at me and Luca.

Luca gave his dad a thumbs up, without taking his arm off of my shoulders. "Got it, *Dad*."

I bit back a laugh, then pulled out from under Luca's warm arm to help unload the supplies we needed for the night from the Turtles. I wanted to get to sleep as soon as possible. The sooner we got this day over with, the sooner we could get on our way again.

"Listen," Hugh said, fiddling with a radio.

"USHA is doing everything in its power to find the missing girl. Chip Sinclair, the director of USHA, said that while the Storm Chasers have never been this violent before, he is not surprised to see that they have escalated their tactics to kidnapping. Ashlyn Booker has long brown hair, although her captors may have altered her appearance. If you have any information on Ashlyn's or the Storm Chasers' whereabouts, please reach out to your local authorities. There is a reward for information leading to the recovery of Ashlyn Booker."

Hugh switched off the radio, and the room was silent as everyone stared at me.

Had I made this dangerous mission worse?

CHAPTER 8

THE SOUND OF TAPPING on metal woke me out of a deep sleep. My eyes were gritty and heavy, and my body told me it hadn't had enough rest.

Ginger stood near the stove and tapped on the pipe with a fire poker. She had turned on two of the lanterns to low power. Everyone stirred in their bunks.

"Sorry, guys." She wore a pained expression. "But we have to leave. I've been watching the radar all night, and there is a break in the band of thunderstorms that will only last for another hour or two. We need to go."

Jack sat up in the bunk above Luca, his hair sticking straight out to the side. "What time is it?"

"Four. I know we said we would sleep until six and roll out at seven, but we need to go now."

I clutched my blanket to my chest, even though I was fully clothed. There's something very vulnerable about waking up with people. I glanced across the room at Luca. Tyler had made sure that Miri and I were as far away as possible from Luca and Jack. As if we were going to try anything in an open room with a bunch of other people sleeping within sight of each other.

Luca rubbed the back of his neck, and he gave me a sleepy grin. Butterflies kicked up a storm in my chest, and heat crawled up my cheeks. I ran my fingers through my hair, still surprised it was short. I used hair ties to put my hair into the two low buns on the back of my head that I had worn yesterday. It was the best way to tie it up, knowing how much wind I was going to face today.

Miri hopped down from the bunk above me, looking like she had had a week's rest.

"How do you do that?" I asked.

She didn't stop rolling up her sleeping bag. "What?"

"Look perfect when you first wake up."

She gave me a side glance. "You tell me."

My mouth dropped open. "I do not. It usually takes me an hour to get ready."

She rolled her eyes. "Well, you've been wasting hours then, because you don't need it. Besides, Luca doesn't care about that stuff."

My eyes widened, and my cheeks warmed. "Luca?"

Miri stopped stuffing her bag and turned to face me. "You know, the hottie over there who can't stop staring at you?"

I had wanted to figure out what was going on between Miri and Luca, but I had thought it would be something I would talk with Luca about. I had never planned on talking to Miri.

I swallowed hard and leaned closer to her, keeping my voice low. "There's nothing going on between us."

She narrowed her eyes. "Whatever, Booker. Just be honest. I don't care, okay? But I hate when things are unsaid and undefined."

I wasn't sure what to say about that. "We don't have anything said or defined to talk about. I broke up with my boyfriend a few weeks ago, and Luca's been a good friend, and I—"

She held up her hand. "You know what? I'm sorry. I didn't mean to force anything. Sorry. I'm too blunt sometimes."

Compassion filled my chest, and I remembered why I liked Miri. I always loved being around people who weren't afraid to say what they were thinking. It was why I was such good friends with Dasha. "Don't be sorry. I'm sorry that I came into this group and made things weird. Luca told me you and he have been friends for a long time."

Her face brightened a little. "He did?"

I nodded. "He said you have been a great friend to him forever. That you've covered his butt more times than he can count. And I was excited to get to know you, but I know I need to take it easy and not expect any deep friendships right away. It takes time to be friends."

Miri gave a ghost of a smile. "You didn't make things weird. You came to find your dad. We're cool."

"We are?"

She rolled her eyes, which made me feel better. I liked it best when she was being her gruff, no nonsense self. "Yes. Now, enough kumbaya. Pack up."

A food bar hit me in the chest and fell to the ground. I glanced around the room to find the assailant. Luca was smiling as Ginger handed out food bars to the rest of the group.

"Nice catch, Booker." He held up his food bar in victory.

I rolled my eyes as I bent over and picked mine up. "Throwing things at unsuspecting people doesn't count as a victory for you, Denzio."

"Less flirting, more packing," Tyler growled. I rolled my eyes at that too, as I opened my bar and shoved one end into my mouth. It tasted like someone was trying to describe peanut butter without knowing what peanut butter tasted like.

Hugh laughed at my face. "They take getting used to. But they have every essential nutritional component, so choke it down."

My face warmed as I realized that everyone in the room was watching me. Apparently, I had missed the training the Storm Chasers had taken on Mission Cuisine. I took a swig of water to help wash the chalky grit down my throat, then took another bite to prove to the group that I could do it. Hugh winked at me, then went back to his stuff.

Packing up didn't take very long, but the line for our makeshift bathroom slowed us all down. We all huddled near the door and tried to talk among ourselves while each person took a turn behind the curtain. I kept letting other people go ahead of me as I worked up the courage to do what I needed to do in a room full of people.

At last, it was down to Ginger and me. She slipped behind the curtain while Tyler barked for everyone to load up the Turtles. He pulled open the door, and we stepped out into the carport. The wind seemed to have died down, but it was hard to tell looking out into the pitch black field surrounding the shelter. Tyler and Silas hit buttons on the side of the Turtles, and they hummed to life, their headlights giving us the light we needed to navigate around. Ginger was right; it wasn't raining right now.

Ginger came out of the shelter and tapped my shoulder. "You're up, Ashlyn."

I nodded. "I'll be fast. Don't let Tyler leave without me."

She grinned. "Don't worry. He's a real curmudgeon, but he also is not the kind to leave someone behind. He's actually a great leader."

I looked over as Tyler gave Miri one of the scowls he usually reserved for me, but then grabbed a heavy pack from her hands and shoved it into one of the storage compartments on the side of the Turtle. Miri turned her back, and Tyler gave a brief grin. That surprised me. Was he just putting on an act?

I hurried into the empty shelter and went behind the curtain. My strategy had worked; I could do my business in an empty room, while everyone else settled themselves in the Turtles. I tried to hurry, but the solitude felt good for a few minutes. I hadn't had a moment alone since we started this trip, which meant I hadn't had time to process everything.

A lump formed in my throat as I finished up behind the curtain. I was still upset about how I left things with Dasha. I wondered if she was having fun in Seattle, or if I had completely ruined the trip for her. And for a moment, I wondered how Mom was doing. It had been almost forty-eight hours since I said goodbye to her. But then I shoved that aside. I couldn't let myself think about her at all. I wished there was a way to get word to her that I was okay, but I couldn't think of how to do it without giving away our position.

I took a deep breath and rubbed hand sanitizer onto my hands, then made my way outside. Luca and Miri stood side by side at the edge of the carport with their backs to me, their hands in the air.

I laughed as I walked toward them. "What Storm Chasers ritual did I miss?"

"Freeze!"

My heart dropped as I stepped out from behind Luca. An armored van blocked the entrance to the carport, and three soldiers stood in the light of Turtles' headlights. Ginger, Sybil, and Hugh sat on the ground with their hands on the back of their heads, and one soldier had his rifle trained on them. The other two soldiers had rifles pointed at us. Silas and Tyler stood with their hands in the air next to the front Turtle.

"You all need to sit down." A soldier with a bushy mustache gestured with his rifle. Miri and Jack sat down, but I stood frozen, half behind Luca.

Silas kept his hands above his head, but did not sit. "Are we under arrest?"

Bushy Mustache let out a laugh. "Uh, yeah. You are not authorized to be in the Disaster Zone. Did you think you could just hang out here?"

The second soldier took a step closer to me and gave me an intense stare. He was taller and broader than the other two, and fear clenched my belly. "What's your name?"

"Don't answer that," Tyler barked. "We don't have to answer any of your questions. The US military doesn't have authority to arrest or detain."

Tall Soldier cocked his rifle. "We do, by order of Chip Sinclair and the United States Hurricane Agency. In case you couldn't tell, you are within the bounds of the hurricane zone, which means you checked your rights at the border."

Bushy Mustache studied my face. "We're looking for a girl who looks like you. Or, you look like her if you did a bad dye job on your hair."

The fear in my belly turned into a rock. I never thought Chip would send someone into the storm to get me. I had felt safe from him once we left the city limits. That he had used his power to send others into danger just to get me back told me everything I needed to know about the lengths he'd go to get what he wanted. There was no way he did this out of the kindness of his heart for me or my mom. I looked at Luca, who pressed his lips together and he opened his eyes wide, as if he was trying to tell me to keep my mouth shut.

"Pretty sure you're not allowed to comment on the appearance of a girl," Miri said, a dark look on her face. "I mean, you can, but the media will have a heyday when I tell them how you treat women."

"Hold on," Silas said, still standing with his hands above his head. "We're not hurting anyone at all. And there's three of you and nine of us. Just let us go, okay? We'll leave you a pack of food, and you can hang out in this nice, warm, dry shelter."

"Sit. Down." Tall Soldier took a step toward Silas.

"We *all* have to go," Ginger said from her seat on the ground. "This break in the thunderstorms isn't going to last much longer. Have you traveled through one of the storms yet? It's dangerous and brutal. We all need to leave now."

"We are all leaving, Sweetheart," Bushy Mustache said. "All of us in our van. There's plenty of room for you all in the back."

"That's a terrible vehicle for this area," Hugh said. "You should ask ol' Chip to get you one of these Turtles. They're perfect; low and heavy, with wide tires to go over debris. I'm surprised he let you in here in those junkers. They're way too tall. You're going to get blown off the road."

"Shut up! If you don't comply, we are authorized to use lethal force." The soldier with his gun on Hugh raised his gun as if he were going to hit Hugh with it.

At that point, pandemonium broke loose. A deafening crack echoed under the carport, and I involuntarily covered my ears. Two more cracks sounded, as Tyler and Silas stood with guns pointed at the soldiers. Where had those guns come from? An acrid, burning stench filled the area as Luca dove on top of me, crashing us both to the ground. The soldiers fired back, the sound of four more shots filling the small space. I tried to close my eyes, but they stayed open. I watched as Miri and Jack crawled behind the Turtle, and Tyler and Silas ran for the other side of the Turtle, both firing off shots. Then the sky lit up with lightning, followed by the low rumbling boom of thunder, as if Goliath wanted to get in on the fire fight.

Just as suddenly as it started, it was over, and I could only hear the rushing wind outside the carport. Luca was still covering me, his breathing heavy. I pushed him away.

All three soldiers were on the ground, blood pooling beneath their bodies. I stood up and walked over to them as if drawn by a magnet. Bushy Mustache stared with wide, lifeless eyes, his face pale as a ghost. The blood spread out in a dark circle beneath him.

"Dad!"

I tore my eyes away from the dead soldier as Luca dove toward Tyler. Tyler laid still on the cement floor of the carport next to the Turtle.

Blood spread out from underneath him too.

CHAPTER 9

"ALL CLEAR!"

No one moved after Silas barked out the command. It was too soon to make such a definitive statement. It felt like minutes passed, but it was only seconds before Ginger popped up from her position behind the Turtle.

"Where did those guns come from? Silas, why do you and Tyler have guns?" Her face was a thundercloud. She had always been calm and steady, even when describing the horrors of the hurricane. In that instant, she appeared as though she might crack.

Silas tucked his gun in the front of his pants. "We brought them in case something like this happened." He walked over to the soldier nearest to Hugh and Ginger. He kicked the gun away from the soldier's hand before bending down to check on him.

Sybil rushed to Bushy Mustache's side and put him on his back. She looked like she was preparing to do CPR. Hugh grabbed her by the shoulders and pulled her back. "They're gone."

She scowled at him. "Oh, you're the medic now? Then why am I here?"

"Not to save them."

Miri and Jack had cautiously emerged from behind their Turtle.

"Oh my gosh, Tyler!" Miri dashed out from behind the Turtle and ran over to where Luca was crouched on the ground next to his dad. It was as if the other adults finally noticed that Tyler had been hit.

I snapped out of my frozen state and rushed to Luca's side. Miri pressed her hands on the wound on Tyler's abdomen without a thought. "Ashlyn, get me a cloth or something to pack this wound." I looked around as Jack ran over, shirtless. He handed me his shirt, and I gave it to Miri, who released the pressure to grab the shirt. The minute she let go, blood soaked his shirt at an alarming rate. Miri tore at Tyler's shirt, exposing the wound before shoving Jack's shirt into the hole the size of a nickel near Tyler's belly button.

Jack ran to the edge of the carport, leaned over, and vomited. I couldn't stop staring at the blood. Sybil dropped to her knees next to Miri, a kit in hand. She pulled out a pouch and ripped it open.

"On the count of three, move the cloth, Miri. I'll dump in this coagulating powder, then you go right back to packing and pressure. Can you handle that?"

Miri nodded, her eyes bright with adrenaline. The plan worked like Sybil had said, and Miri had her hands back on Tyler's abdomen within ten seconds.

"Dad? Dad." Luca kneeled near Tyler's head, and patted his face. Up to this point, Tyler had been as still as the soldiers; the only sign of life had been the blood gushing from the wound in his abdomen.

Tyler groaned and shifted. "What? Luca?"

"Keep him still," Sybil barked as she dug in the med kit.

Luca pressed on Tyler's shoulders with his hands, pinning him in place. "Don't move, Dad. Sybil will get you patched up, but I don't think moving around is going to help."

Tyler's face turned a ghostly shade of white, all traces of grumpiness gone. "That's why she's on this mission; she's the best."

Sybil grabbed my arm, and I tore my eyes away from Tyler to look at her. "Ashlyn, we need blankets. I've got one emergency blanket here, but we need more. We've got to keep him warm to prevent him from going into shock."

I raced for my pack and dug out my sleeping bag. It was amazing that something that could fold down to the size of a soda can could stretch out and be so warm. Hugh tossed me his as well, and I ran back to Sybil.

"He's in shock. He needs blood to his brain," Miri was saying.

Sybil looked firm. "I am aware he's in shock, but we're not going to raise his legs. We don't know where that bullet is inside him, or how close it is to his spine."

Miri scowled while still keeping pressure on Tyler's wound. "Who cares about his spine? If he's brain dead, it won't matter if he can walk or not."

I unfolded the sleeping bags and laid them out over Tyler. It was awkward, since Miri couldn't move. I tucked them in around his shoulders and under his legs without trying to jostle him too much.

Tyler opened his eyes and gave a small smile. "It's weird hearing you all talk about me. I'm awake."

Sybil reached up and smoothed the hair away from Tyler's forehead. "Good. Stay awake, okay? And chime in. We want your opinion, too."

Tyler tried to swallow, but it looked as if the effort was going to make him pass out. Luca grabbed his water bottle and tried to trickle a little in Tyler's mouth without making him move too much.

"I do have an opinion," Tyler said. "You've got to let me go."

My mouth dropped open and every person around him protested.

"Dad, come on. Don't be an idiot." Luca leaned down so his face was inches away from Tyler's. "We'll rest here, then get you back to Tennessee."

Tyler tried to shake his head, but only managed to blink slowly. "Son, I'm freezing and my head is spinning. Miri can't keep her hands on me forever. Plus, you saw how long it took to get here. There's no way I can make it back."

Luca looked angry. "Sybil, tell him."

Tears had filled Sybil's eyes. "Luca, I'm so sorry. But he's right. He would need to be in surgery in, like, ten minutes. But he's lost too much blood, and I can't do anything about the bullet inside him. If we move him, the bullet might shift, which would make him bleed faster."

I couldn't believe what I was hearing. What year was this? People didn't die of these kinds of injuries anymore, did they? We had come so far in our medical advances. I had read about what it was like when people would bleed out on the streets after car crashes, but our first aid kits had come a long way. That powder Sybil used should have been enough to stop the bleeding.

"Dad, hang in there," Luca pleaded. "If you promise to hang on, I'll buy the tacos for the rest of our lives, okay? Anytime you want."

Tyler swallowed and tried to smile. "Son."

"We've got more than one first aid kit, don't we?" I jumped up. "Tell me where it is, and we can use another packet. That'll get him ready to move, right?"

Tyler smiled at me. That smile alone scared me more than anything I had seen so far. It was so out of character that I felt certain something bad was about to happen.

"Booker, no. I refuse treatment."

Luca shook his head. "You don't have the right to refuse treatment, Dad. Ashlyn, go get the kit."

Tyler shook his head more forcefully, then groaned and coughed. I sank back to my knees. I didn't want him hurting himself. "Son, I do have the right. You all may need what's in those kits for the rest of the mission. I will not let you waste them on me."

"Rest of the mission? We can't finish this mission. We're going back." Luca re-tucked the sleeping bag around Tyler's shoulders, as if the sleeping bag was the difference between life and death.

Tyler looked at Sybil, and they seemed to have a conversation with their eyes. Sybil gave a sad smile and nodded as she reached down and squeezed Tyler's hand. He gave a weak squeeze back, then looked at the rest of us.

"Can I have a moment with my son?"

I looked at the adults. Ginger, Hugh, and Silas were standing over us, their arms folded and faces filled with sorrow. One by one, they bent over and touched Tyler on the arm or leg before walking to the other side of the carport.

Miri shook her head. "No way. I move, you die. I'm not letting up."

Tyler gave a weak chuckle. "Fine, you can stay. Just look away, okay?" She nodded, then squeezed her eyes shut tight and turned her head without letting up on the pressure.

I moved to get up when Tyler called my name.

"Booker. Wait. I'm sorry I was so hard on you. If it wasn't for you and what you did for us back at USHA headquarters, we wouldn't have been able to come down here. And I know you want to find your dad. Good luck, okay?"

I couldn't speak around the lump in my throat, so I nodded. I looked at Luca, but he had his eyes fixed on his dad.

Making myself get up and walk over to the rest of the group was the hardest thing I had ever done. I wanted to stay with Luca. He needed someone with him right then. And to be honest, I was battling jealousy that Miri was the one who got to be there for him.

But that was stupid. I tried to put that thought out of my head. Miri had already been with the Denzios through thick and thin, so of course she should be there for this part. I was still the outsider, and I had no rights to anything.

I joined the group, expecting to find them solemn and sad. Instead, a heated discussion was going on.

"Are you kidding me?" Jack had folded his arms across his bare chest, and he was shivering. "We can't leave."

Ginger gave him a look of compassion. "We have to. We should have left thirty minutes ago. We're still in the window to make it to the eye. That's the mission."

Silas shrugged off his jacket and put it around Jack's shoulders. "Tyler wants us to complete the mission. That is our priority. We all understood this was dangerous, right? We all knew that there was a possibility that someone might not make it."

Rage filled my chest. "You knew it was a possibility that someone would get shot by the American military?"

Silas shook his head, then shrugged. "Not specifically, but we thought we might come up against hostile forces. Tyler and I figured it would be closer to the eye. Or inside the eye."

I clenched my fists. "When were you going to share that with the rest of us?"

Ginger touched my arm. "Ashlyn, I know you're new to the Storm Chasers. This is something we usually talk about at length. I'm sorry we didn't brief you before, but to be honest, we didn't think to rehash it. Would it have changed your mind about coming?"

I tried to slow my breathing as I thought about what she said. I glanced over my shoulder; Luca had his head close to Tylers, and Miri still had her eyes shut and her face turned away. Miri's shoulders were shaking. "No. I would have still come."

Silas put his hand on my shoulder. "If you want to find your dad, this is our window. A window like this won't come for another ten years."

I swallowed hard. "So we're just going to leave? What about Tyler?"

Sybil set the first aid kit on the ground. "I'll take Tyler back to Tennessee."

"How?"

"In the van. We just have to find the keys."

The sky outside the carport was beginning to lighten up. As light as possible with the heavy storm clouds, anyway. There wasn't much vegetation to blow around, but the wind rushing past the shelter sounded like a freight train. It wasn't raining, but that was likely to change any second.

"You'll have to clear the roads by yourself."

Sybil nodded. "Maybe it won't be so bad, since we cleared them yesterday."

Ginger had a tech pad out and tapped on the screen. "The weather to the north looks pretty clear. The forecast model shows storms developing later today. So the sooner you can go, the better."

Sybil handed the first aid kit and her pack to Hugh. "Would you radio Jim? He's the one on duty at headquarters in Murfreesboro, right? Tell him I'm coming. I won't leave until it's time."

A rock formed in my stomach as I realized what she meant by "time." She would not move Tyler in this condition, which meant that she was going to wait for his condition to change. And there was only one way that his condition was going to go.

Miri stepped up next to me, her face streaked with tears and her hands covered in blood. "He's gone."

CHAPTER 10

I TRIED TO MAKE eye contact with Miri, but she climbed back into the Turtle without looking at me. She touched Luca's shoulder, and he sighed. My stomach tightened. When I reached out to him, he acted like I wasn't even there.

Luca hadn't said a word. He stayed motionless in his spot in the front passenger seat of the Turtle, even when Silas got into Tyler's seat and took over driving. Miri and I took on the extra work to help clear the roads every time we stopped. Luca seemed to either stare out the window at the rain blowing sideways, or to be asleep.

Of course, I didn't blame him. I can't imagine what I would have done if I had been holding my dad's hand when he passed away. I'm not sure I would ever forget the heartbreaking sight of Luca standing up, walking to the Turtle, and buckling himself in without a word.

I desperately wanted to talk to Miri about what happened, but there was no opportunity. The wind was too loud outside when we got out of the Turtle for road clearing duty, and the seats in the Turtle were too close together to even whisper without being overheard. But she also didn't seem to want to talk about it.

I tried to be understanding. She held her hands on Tyler's stomach until he took his last breath. And she had known

Tyler and Luca for a long time. However, she seemed to be a robot in go-mode. As if putting pressure on Tyler's mortal wound while he said his goodbyes to his son was just another one of her daily tasks for the Storm Chasers.

For the ten thousandth time, I wondered if I made the right choice coming on this mission. I had been so naïve. I thought we'd be driving through the wind to get to the Eye, and then I'd find my dad. Or not. But we'd be there. Never in my wildest dreams did I imagine that we'd be on the run from the military, or that I would see dead bodies in real life. Or that one of *us* would die.

I could have gone back with Sybil. I could have slept in the warm bed in Murfreesboro and gotten more tacos at that restaurant near the train station. I could have called Mom and let her know I was alright, and that I was coming home.

But I would have had to ride with Tyler's body. And it would have meant giving up the chance to see *my* dad. I reminded myself that it wasn't a guarantee that I would find Dad at the end of this journey, but not finishing it meant I wouldn't find him at all.

I pulled down my goggles and tightened my hood around my face as we stopped again. These rain jumpsuits had turned out to be life-savers. The driving rain was turning my cheeks raw, but at least my clothes were dry. And the heater in the Turtle was nice.

"The shelter in Tifton is not very far from here," Silas said before we jumped out of the Turtle. "It's a mile and a half that way."

I glanced at Luca, whose eyes were closed. Then I got out and got to work. The sooner we got this road cleared, the sooner we would stop.

The wind and debris seemed a lot worse at this point. It was strong all day, but this time felt more sinister. Every branch we moved was replaced as soon as we hauled it off the road. I stumbled more than once because the wind seemed to be determined to knock me down, before getting the hang of keeping my knees bent and leaning into the wind. I was grateful that Silas and Tyler had made us get used to clipping in before leaving the Turtles. The wind made it take twice as long to clear this stretch of highway as it had anywhere else.

My arms were limp by the time I got back in the Turtle, and Silas started our slow crawl over the hill. I almost cried when I saw the shelter in the distance. If it weren't for the hills, Georgia would have looked like Eastern Colorado; nothing but brown fields in every direction. Goliath had shredded and ripped all the trees and shrubs down to kindling decades ago and now seemed content to toss the sticks around in circles for the rest of eternity. The only structure able to survive for this long was one built like this shelter.

Silas lead the way this time, leaving Hugh's Turtle to keep its back end exposed out of the concrete carport. Hugh and Jack pulled thick, heavy chains out of a compartment in the back on the Turtle, and used them to chain the Turtle to the walls of the carport, to give added security against the wind.

I put my hand on Luca's shoulder. "Hey. We can get out. We're here."

He slowly blinked and lifted his head up as if it weighed a hundred pounds. He really had been asleep. He glanced around, but wouldn't look me in the eye. He unbuckled himself and pushed himself out of the seat.

Miri held out a water bottle to him, and he looked at her with a small smile. She gave him the same sad smile, and they climbed out of the Turtle together.

My stomach twisted into a knot. My brain told me he was just grieving. They had experienced something together and might be the best ones to help each other at the moment. But my heart felt bruised and left out. As if he was mad at *me*.

Maybe he had the right to be. If it hadn't been for me and my big mouth, Chip might have never known why the Storm Chasers had broken into his office, and he might never have been alerted to a mission to the eye. He would have just focused on his stupid campaign for the presidency, and trying to prove to my mom that he was a good guy. But I had to call him out. And then he sent the military after us.

I took a deep breath and tried to push those thoughts out of my mind. It was impossible for Chip to follow us this far, so now it was all moot. This journey was grueling, and we all needed to do our part to help. Today was a day that I could do a lot of the work, to give Luca and even Miri the space they needed to process what happened this morning. If it meant being the pack horse, then that's what I would do.

The shelter was much bigger than the one in Macon. There was even a walled, separate bathroom with a shower. Something told me the water in the shower would be cold, but I didn't care. I was thrilled to see an actual door.

Jack was hooting and pumping his fist in the air at the sight of a large stack of dry wood next to a black stove. I dropped the packs in surprise.

"Dry wood? How is that possible?"

Ginger lugged a bulky trunk into the shelter. "I wonder how long that's been there. I mean, in order to dry like that, it must have been here for years."

Hugh grinned. "Who wants to learn how to build a fire?" Jack raised his hand, and the two of them got to work.

Luca and Miri had gone directly to the bunks. Luca had already laid down with his face to the wall. Miri sat on the floor next to his bed, her head in her hands. It was the first time all day that she had looked wiped out.

I grabbed their packs and took them over. I was still at a loss at what to do. Miri gave me a sad look and shrugged her shoulders. I peeled out of my rain jumpsuit and held out my hand to her. She stood, took off hers, and handed me the wet material. She then sat on the foot of Luca's bed, her back to the wall.

Someone had strung several strings across the width of the shelter. Ginger had already draped her rain jumpsuit over one to dry, so I did the same with mine and Miri's. Everything about this cabin felt like we had been transported back to the pioneer days. Well, except for the battery powered lanterns, and the tech pads Ginger had pulled out.

Silas came in with one more crate of gear, then pushed the heavy door shut. The shrieking wind could barely be heard once the door was closed, and I was never more glad for silence.

"This is it. This is the edge of Goliath." Ginger turned her tech pad around, and we crowded around the table. The green dot that showed where we were was sitting on a blue band that outlined the same image I had seen of Goliath my whole life. I had a hard time wrapping my mind around the fact that I was there. The blue and green portions of the image were very thin. Our path took us through them, through the thicker yellow ring, and directly into the bright red center.

"What is that?" I asked, pointing to a black ring surrounding the eye. "Why is it black?"

"You've never seen a black eye?" Jack asked, a goofy look on his face.

"That's the eyewall." Ginger zoomed in on that part of the image. The black circle looked as if someone had drawn a map around the entire city of Orlando. "It's the ring of clouds around the eye, where the winds are the strongest. And Goliath is about to enter an eyewall replacement cycle. That's when the outer bands strengthen and group together to become a ring of thunderstorms, which makes a new outer eyewall. This red band will turn to a dark maroon, if that makes sense. Then it overtakes the first eyewall, causing it to collapse."

I swallowed hard. "When will that happen?"

Ginger tapped on her tech pad. "The good news is, the model hasn't changed in the last five days, so I'm confident enough to say that the process will probably start on Monday. The bad news is, according to our data, Goliath's eyewall replacement cycle only takes twelve hours to complete. That means we need to breach the eye before it starts."

"Or we could be blown off the face of the earth," Jack said.

Ginger gave a tight, nervous smile. "Let's just say we don't want even the Turtles caught in the middle of that process."

I stared at the tech pad. "So you're sure about how long it'll take to replace?"

She nodded. "It's one more piece of evidence we have that Goliath is man-made. It has to be. It is following patterns that aren't natural. No storm should be able to be scheduled and tracked. I mean, once they form, we can predict how they will act, but since Goliath is fifty years old, we can not only predict the patterns, we can say for sure what happens when."

Silas had been standing near the table this whole time, his arms crossed. "Which means we are on a tight schedule. And can't afford dead weight."

My mouth dropped open as everyone glanced around, avoiding looking at of the bunks.

"You might as well just say what you want," Miri growled from her spot next to Luca. "Like, why are you beating around the bush?"

Silas sighed. "Okay, fine. Luca, we need to know your plan. Are you good to move on? Or do you need to stay?"

Luca shifted a little, but kept his back to the rest of us.

My heart broke for him. "Come on. This isn't fair."

Silas walked over to Luca's bed, crouched down, and put his hand on Luca's shoulder. "Son, I'm not trying to be rude. But you understand better than any of us that the timing is critical. You were a part of every single planning meeting that your dad was in. I'm so sorry, but what do you want to do? I'm not saying you need to come. Stay here and set up the communication equipment, and monitor our activity.

We had hoped to set up a communications relay, anyway. We would pick you up on the way back."

Luca rolled over and had no expression on his face. "No. I want to go."

Miri's mouth dropped open. "Seriously?"

Luca pushed himself into a sitting position, his feet on the floor. "Yeah. I'm serious. I'm good. I'm sorry about today, guys. But I'm good to go now. It's what Dad and I planned, so I have to see it through. For him."

We all stared at him, and the room seemed silent. I could tell that the adults wanted to intervene, but after a few minutes, they each nodded. Luca was over eighteen, after all. He was able to make his own choice.

Silas kept his eyes on Luca's. "You're sure? You're ready to pitch in and do what it takes?"

He nodded. "Yes. I'm sure. I won't let you down."

Silas put his hand back on Luca's shoulder. "I know you won't." His voice was choked, and he stood quickly and walked back to the crates of gear. Ginger, Silas, Hugh, and Jack all huddled around the crate filled with equipment and started pulling things out and talking through what to do next.

Miri got up from her spot next to Luca and headed for the bathroom. It was the first time all day that she left his side.

I sat down next to him, leaving a few inches between us. "How are you?" I knew it was a dumb question, but it seemed better than asking him if he was okay.

He looked at me, his eyes shadowed. "I wish I knew what to say. I just know I don't have any more time to deal with that. I need to concentrate on the mission."

I scooted closer to him. "Are you sure?"

He leaned in. "Yeah. Because Dad's last words to me were 'find out how they found us.' He meant those military guys. There's no way they should have shown up at that exact shelter. Which means someone tipped them off. And I have to find out what's going on. For Dad."

CHAPTER 11

The door to the shelter banged open, and I let out an involuntary shriek. I tried to cover my mouth before it slipped out, but I couldn't help it.

Silas had drawn his gun and pointed it at the intruder. Luca jumped up and also had a gun pointed at the door. He must have taken Tyler's gun.

A tall, wet figure stood in the doorway, hands raised. They were wearing the same rain jumpsuit we all had, and had goggles covering most of their face. "Whoa, sorry! It's just me!"

Silas kept his gun up. "We weren't expecting any 'me,' so you'll have to do better than that."

The person slowly moved their hands to push back their goggles. The slow motion was almost comical. A young man peeked out, his eyes wide. Once the googles were on top of his head, he put his hands back in the air.

"Sorry! So sorry! I'm Reuben. I'm with the Storm Chasers? You guys are too, right?"

I felt a little sorry for Reuben. His face looked as wet and chapped as the rest of ours, and he clearly had not expected to walk into a room where people would be pointing guns at him.

Silas still had his gun trained on Reuben. "Who sent you?"

Reuben breathed fast. "Matteo, man! Matteo! But he said you'd be here yesterday, but you weren't, so I thought I'd go get some more stuff for you guys, because that trip in is brutal man. I mean, I haven't even been out of the storm for six years now, but I remember what it was like. So I brought you all the wood yesterday, which was so hard because it was heavy and I'm a little guy. But I thought you'd want a warm shelter, and no one has used this shelter in about three years. But warmth is life in Goliath, man. Am I right?"

He was rambling and his teeth chattered. The wind pushing in from the open door reminded me how cold it was. We had already gotten used to the warmth of the room, and the open door was letting all the heat out.

"Silas." Ginger gave him a look, and Silas put down his gun. Luca did too. Reuben kept one hand in the air, but stepped back outside and bent over to grab the handle of a chest. He looked so funny, with the one hand up, trying to drag something that was very heavy. Jack ran over and helped him pull it into the room, and then slammed the door shut again.

Miri came out of the bathroom and stopped short. "Whoa! Who are you?"

Silas pointed at a chair and Reuben sat. "This is Reuben. He says he's with the Storm Chasers and Matteo sent him, but I've never heard of him."

Ginger rolled her eyes. "Can he at least get out of that wet jumpsuit?"

Silas scowled and nodded. Reuben shot a grateful smile to Ginger, then jumped up and peeled out of his jumpsuit in a way that told me he had done it a thousand times. He ran it to the bathroom. "You gotta squeeze them out first, in the shower or toilet or something, or they'll never dry overnight. Trust me. Putting on a damp jumpsuit is very unpleasant."

I looked at the puddle of water under our jumpsuits and mentally smacked myself. Why hadn't I thought of that? I pulled down all our jumpsuits off the line and headed into the bathroom to squeeze them out. I kept the door open, though, because I wanted to hear Reuben's story.

"Man, you look just like Matteo. I mean, a younger version of him. Is he older? Or did the storm life, like, age him faster? It's hard to tell. Living in the storm is not for the faint of heart, but we're glad to do it because of this day. You're finally here! We were thinking this would never happen." Reuben hardly stopped to breathe between any of his words. I couldn't tell if this was normal for him, or if he was still freaked out from having a gun pulled on him.

Silas held up his hand, and Reuben stopped talking. "I need more proof that you know Matteo."

Reuben didn't hide the fear from his face. "Oh yeah! Sure, sure. Um, let's see, I met Matteo on the outside, like, seven years ago. You know, before he came in the storm? I had gone to one of his Storm Chaser meetings in Nashville, even though my mom said they were dumb and probably some kind of pyramid scheme. But what he said made so much sense! And he said he was building a team to go inside Goliath, because he had gotten hold of all these plans for shelters. I mean, how did they know to build these kinds of shelters? It's shady stuff, man. Like someone *knew* Goliath was coming. Which is crazy, because that was fifty years ago, and, like they barely had the internet or something back then. But Matteo believed that someday we'd be able to get to the eye, and then we could blow this sucker wide open. But the storm has been so bad. Like, what you see now is like a nice, breezy rainstorm compared to what it's been like. But I wanted to join that team, and so I came with Matteo."

Hugh looked at Silas. "And Matteo never mentioned him?"

Silas kept his eye on Reuben. "No. But I guess he never told me the names of the entire team. And our communication has always been real short messages."

"That's cause Goliath knocks out all the signals, man!" Reuben said. "But Matteo said you were bringing equipment to help. Like, stuff that might boost the signal up above Goliath to the satellites. Did you?"

"Oh yeah," Jack said. "Check out this stuff. We stole it from USHA, so it's gotta work."

That was news to me. I had no idea that there had been any other raids on USHA. Of course, USHA had other facilities than their headquarters in Colorado Springs. I bet they stole all the gear we were using.

"You satisfied?" Ginger asked Silas.

He narrowed his eyes. "Almost. I will be if he can describe Matteo's tattoo."

Reuben let out a laugh. "Which one, man? My favorite is the dolphin on his bicep. It's hilarious. Like, did he get that one for a girl? He said he was nineteen, but there's no way he could have picked that out on his own."

Silas relaxed and smiled. "Yeah, I'm satisfied."

Reuben sank back into his chair, the relief on his face making him look ten years younger. "Oh good. I'm so sorry, man. I should have left a note with the wood or something."

Hugh glanced at Luca, who had put his gun away and was sitting on his bed. "It took us longer than we planned once we left Murfreesboro, so we ended up stopping at a shelter in Macon. We ran into some trouble there, so we don't really appreciate being surprised by people."

Reuben's eyes opened wide. "Whoa, the Macon shelter? Nobody has used that one in years. I mean, most of them haven't, but that's the one we stay away from. It's like a trap. Somehow, the military watches it. Hey, where's Tyler Denzio? Matteo wouldn't shut up about Silas and Tyler like they were some dynamic duo. Did he not come?"

I looked at Luca, whose face flinched. I jumped in, trying to protect him. "Tyler didn't make it."

Reuben wrinkled his forehead. "Did he get sick? Matteo missed a mission once because of a sinus infection. That bites, man. But what can you do when you have a window you gotta make it through?"

Luca stood up. "No, the military killed him in Macon."

Reuben's mouth dropped open, and he was silent for a few seconds. "Oh gosh. I'm so sorry, dude."

Luca shrugged. "I'll deal with that later. Right now, we've got a mission to complete."

The rest of the team took that a signal to carry on with the preparations for the next leg. Ginger continued her study of the radar images, trying to determine what time we needed to leave in order to have the most optimal trip to the shelter in Valdosta. Hugh and Jack sorted through the com equipment to find the pieces they needed to set up and leave behind. Silas and Miri opened up the chest Reuben brought to check out the supplies.

Once again, I felt like the spare part. I didn't have a particular job to do, and I hated that. I glanced at Luca, who was pulling things out of his pack. I decided to set up my bunk, then hang out with Ginger. At least I could learn about the storm.

"Whoa, is this fresh bread?" Miri's voice rang out across the shelter, and everyone stopped what they were doing.

"Yep." Reuben looked proud. "Well, it was baked within the last week. If you toast it over the stove, and spread this strawberry jam on it, it tastes okay."

Silas narrowed his eyes. "Did you bake it?"

Reuben's smile faltered. "Uh, no. I don't cook. At least, not if you want actual food to eat. But don't worry, our team made it, so it's not poisoned."

"We weren't worried about poison," Silas said.

"We just want to know how your team is able to bake bread. Or have flour. I thought none of Matteo's team had left the storm in years," Hugh said.

"I mean, we get supplies. Did Matteo tell you that? We gotta have food to live." Reuben was chattering again. "Wait'll you see the shelter in Gainesville. It is tricked out. Like, there's a hydroponics farm and everything. We gotta gal who loves to grow things and cook stuff."

I stepped closer to Luca and spoke in a low voice. "I know I'm new to the Storm Chasers, but this seems shady. Is this legit?"

Luca kept his eyes on Reuben. "I don't know. I've never heard anything about hydroponics. The only thing I've ever heard Dad and Silas talk about was how Matteo would raid the supply shipments that were headed to the Eye. I assumed it meant they took the pod meals and new rain jumpsuits."

Silas grinned at Reuben. "Well, thanks to our new friend, we have some excellent dessert to go with our beef stew pods tonight."

Jack groaned. "Man, that beef stew repeats on me."

Miri wrinkled her nose. "Oh gross."

Reuben grinned. "I got something for that too! Activated charcoal tablets. Homemade, but they work great."

Silas walked toward the bathroom, and Luca waved him over. "Do you trust this guy?"

Silas gave a small shrug. "Not completely. But he's got the right answers, and he has stuff that will make our lives easier. I haven't been able to connect with Matteo since we left Tennessee, so I say we just go on with our mission."

"Is he coming with us?" Luca gave a nod in Reuben's direction.

"I'm not sure. I don't even know what kind of vehicle he has. But it sounds like he's been on Matteo's team, which means he might be helpful to us."

Luca folded his arms and narrowed his eyes. "I have one more question. Why is Reuben here, and not Matteo?"

Reuben cleared his throat. "Uh, guys, I can hear you. Like, you gotta really whisper in these shelters if you don't want to be overheard. I just want to tell you that I'm a good guy. Matteo is working on something and will meet you in Gainesville. He sent me to bring you stuff and be your guide."

He reached into his shirt and pulled out a plastic bag, which he handed to Silas. Silas opened the bag and pulled out a small device the size of a pen. He pressed the button on the end. A voice came out of the pen.

"The code to the shelter is 85-4235-57-816. Don't forget the toilet paper this time."

Silas looked at Luca. "That's definitely Matteo. And that is the code I used to get in here."

Reuben laughed. "Yeah, he gave me that because I can never remember codes and stuff. I have, like, no short-term memory. Only long term."

Silas tucked the device in his pocket. "Okay, then. Eat and rest, everyone. I want everyone to get a full eight hours of sleep, which means lights out in three hours."

The team went back to work, and I looked at Luca. He shrugged and returned to his pack.

The heaviness of the day's events eased a bit off of my heart. I couldn't believe our luck. We had an actual guide to help us.

"I'm coming, Dad," I whispered.

Chapter 12

In a different life, we might have described the road the next day as pleasant. We were deep into the flat farmland of Georgia, so all the sticks and branches had blown away years ago. The roads were quite clear, except for a few low spots where the water came up almost to the windshield of the Turtles. But, like Silas had said, the Turtles seemed to be designed for it. No water creeped in through the doors.

The wind and rain slowed us down most. The water blew sideways with such force that it was almost impossible to see very far in front of us. Reuben's little humvee led the way, with our Turtle behind. He had a blinking red light on the back of his humvee, and sometimes that was the only thing we could see.

We had been driving for hours down I-75. In this weather, we were only able to go about ten miles per hour, and that slowed to inches when we hit the flooded areas. Sometimes it didn't look like there was any road at all. As if Goliath had rubbed the concrete and pavement off of the face of the earth. At one point, we had to stop and let Ginger check the GPS. It turned out we had gotten off track and headed east. After that, she radioed she would keep a constant eye on her tech pad.

I hated being so dependent on technology. I couldn't wait to get to the next shelter to find out how Reuben had driven around in the storm all these years. I was a little bored just riding in the Turtle, but Reuben had his hands full driving, so I didn't want to make him tell his story over the radio.

Luca and Miri still weren't talking much. The waiting and sitting made me antsy. I fingered the com Hugh had given me in Murfreesboro. I should have loaded a few videos or some music on it to have for times like this.

Luca pressed the radio button. "Ginger, location check."

A few seconds passed before she responded. "We're on track. We're about ten miles outside of Valdosta. So, about another hour."

"This is the pretty part of Georgia," Reuben piped in. "My grandparents used to live down here."

"Wait, hold on. Silas, stop driving." Ginger's voice had an edge of panic.

Silas stopped the Turtle and grabbed the radio from Luca. "Ginger, report."

"Ah, the pad glitched. It went black, and when it came back on, it looked like we were headed west. But then our GPS dot moved back to I-75."

"What do you mean, moved?"

"The dot moved. It corrected."

"So, are we on track or not?"

Silence.

"I don't know."

Silas hesitated for a moment, then pushed the radio button again. "Reuben, did you hear all that?"

Silence.

I tried to peer out the front window, but it looked like we were sitting directly under a waterfall. The windshield wipers of the Turtle ran at max power, but it was like it wasn't even trying to keep up.

"Where's Reuben? His lights are gone," I said.

Miri frowned. "Did he leave us in the dust?"

Luca was tapping a ferocious beat on the dash. "There's no dust out here."

"Ha ha. I'm serious. Did the weasel take off?"

Panic crawled up my throat. It was almost impossible to see, and our only guide was nowhere to be seen. It hit me like the ninety-mile-an-hour wind gust: this is probably what happened to Dad. Did he have a GPS ten years ago to keep him on the road? Or did he think he'd be fine if he just stayed on the road and underestimated how bad the visibility was? Suddenly my mind was filled with the images of the dead bodies of the soldiers in Macon, only every single one of them had Dad's face.

I tried to take a deep breath, but my breathing was too fast. Luca turned in his seat and looked at me, his eyes filled with concern. "Booker?"

"He's gone, isn't he?"

"No, he's somewhere. He'll realize we're not behind him soon. I'm sure he'll be back."

I shook my head. "No. My dad. There's no way he could have survived this. And now we're lost, just like him."

Luca and Miri glanced at each other, then they both unbuckled and awkwardly crawled over and past each other to switch seats. Luca sat close to me on the bench and took my hand. "Remember the coffee shop in Castle Pines?"

I stared at him. "What are you talking about?"

"Remember the thing that Silas showed you to convince you to help us with the raid on USHA?"

I stared at Luca's and my hands clasped together. My brain felt fuzzy, like all this rain had washed away any coherent thought. It seemed so long ago. I met Luca and Silas at a coffee shop, and I was still so mad at them for asking me to betray my mom by stealing her access card. Luca bought me a chocolate croissant, and I wanted to throw it in his face. Instead, I tried to get my point across by eating it aggressively.

Then Silas pulled out a picture of a log from one shelter inside Goliath. Dad had written his name, and the date was three years ago. Which means he survived for at least seven.

Hope filled my chest and tears spilled down my cheeks. I hated I was a stress crier. I wiped them away. "My dad was alive three years ago."

Luca tightened his grip on my hand and nodded. "And the fact that Reuben is with us tells us that people can survive for years in here. No matter what Goliath throws at them."

I took a deep breath and laid my head on Luca's shoulder. Guilt immediately washed over me. I should have been the one comforting Luca. He had actually lost his dad. Mine was only missing.

"Ginger. Report." Silas' voice carried a biting edge, and he spoke louder than usual.

"I don't know. We should wait."

He let out a loud sigh as he pressed the radio button. "We can't just sit here. We have to move somewhere."

There was silence over the radio for a few minutes.

"This is pointless," Silas said. "I'm going to go over there and find out what's going on."

Miri grunted. "That seems stupid. Like, you might get lost in the rain if you went the wrong direction." She was right; the visibility hadn't changed.

Silas rolled his eyes. "I'll be fine. I'll harness in."

Luca leaned forward. "And if you're not, that means I get to drive this thing?"

That made Silas stop and sigh again. He pressed the button on the radio. "We have to move forward. Let's go another mile or two and check what the GPS does."

Silence, then the radio crackled to life. "Yeah, okay. I guess more data may help us calibrate." Ginger sounded unsure, but I agreed with Silas. We had to go somewhere.

Suddenly, bright lights cut through the rain. Someone was driving directly at us.

"Is that Reuben?" Miri asked.

Silas gripped the wheel and frowned. "Those headlights are way too high. Reuben's vehicle is smaller than that."

The vehicle pulled up next to ours. My heart pounded. "Is that like the van we saw in Macon?"

Luca let go of my hand and pulled out his gun.

Silas pressed the button on the radio. "Hugh, we've got an unknown vehicle next to us. Do you have a visual?"

"No, we can barely see your tail lights."

Fear flooded my veins. Had Chip found us? How? It wasn't possible for him to track us in this storm. My stomach clenched.

"Silas, where did you get your info on the shelter locations?" I asked.

"Matteo. Why?"

"Where did he get it?"

"He came across it back when he and Jonah worked for USHA."

Just like I thought. I was foolish to believe we could escape his wrath, even in the heart of the storm. "So USHA has a record of all these shelters. Which means Chip knows where they are and where to send troops looking for us."

Silas kept his eye on the dark shape outside of his window. "Yeah, I guess."

Through the rain, we saw some movement. A person moved close to the driver's side window and stood for a few seconds with both hands raised. They were covered from head to toe in rain protection gear. No skin was showing. They reached out and tapped on Silas' window before putting their hands back in the raised position.

"I guess that means they're not armed," Miri said.

"Or that they're not holding their gun yet," Silas replied. He pressed a button and lowered the window a half inch. Rain poured in through the opening.

"Hello!" the person shouted over the wind. "We've got shelter two miles that way. It's big enough for your vehicle. Follow us." He pointed back in the direction he came, which was the way we were going.

"Who are you?" Silas demanded.

"You wanna chat in this storm? No thanks. You can follow us or not, but I'm not going to stay in this rain much longer. There's a large concrete garage right on this road, and we can talk there. Or not. It's up to you, but we're leaving in two minutes and that's your window to follow us. If you don't, I can't guarantee that anyone will let you in later." The figure backed away toward their vehicle.

"Wait," Silas shouted. "We have two vehicles this size. If we decide to come, can we both fit?"

"Yeah, of course. Two minutes. Then we're out." The person disappeared into the dark shape of the vehicle.

Silas raised the window and pressed the button on the radio. "Hugh, the person said they have shelter two miles down the road."

"Is that shelter on your map?"

"Negative."

Ginger's voice came over the radio. "We should go. I need a chance to check our equipment, and if they have a dry spot to do it, then we have to."

Silas thought for a minute. "Yeah, okay. They're going to start driving in about a minute, and I'll follow. Stay close behind."

"Got it."

"Ginger, keep an eye on that GPS. We need our location ASAP."

"Yeah, got it, Silas."

The dark shape of the vehicle backed up and made a U turn in front of our Turtle. There were two rows of lights along the base of the vehicle that made it easy to see through the driving rain.

Silas gripped the wheel. "This might be our worst idea yet."

"Maybe. But it's only a couple of miles, right?" Miri asked. "I mean, we could always bail."

"I hope it's only a couple of miles." Silas handed the radio to Miri. "Check in with Hugh. I don't want to do it and drive."

We crawled along behind the vehicle. I had to give them credit; they were going very slowly, which meant they cared that we were able to follow them.

"Do you think these guys found Reuben?" I asked.

Luca's expression darkened. "I'm thinking these guys *know* Reuben."

My mouth dropped open. "Why?"

"How did they know we were here? Like, how did they find us?"

Miri turned around in her seat. "Yeah, I doubt these guys patrol the road, looking for lost souls. Nobody wanders the hurricane."

I bit my lip. "I knew the Storm Chasers were in here. And I guess I should have expected military, based on those supply lists we found at USHA. But I never dreamed we'd meet anyone else."

"That's the problem," Silas said. "We have no intel on who these people are or what they're doing. Or what they want. I need you guys to be on your guard when we get there. Stay close to the Turtle. If anything feels off, jump back in and lock the door. And be prepared to drive away."

A lump formed in my throat. "You mean without the team?"

Silas nodded.

The rain and wind lightened. It didn't stop, but it wasn't so blinding, as if we passed through a gate. The vehicle in front of us was some kind of humvee, but not marked like the military's. A very large concrete parking garage loomed ahead. I could see at least three stories.

A steel gate rolled open as our lead vehicle approached. It disappeared into the darkness.

And Silas followed it.

CHAPTER 13

Driving into the darkness was one of the scariest things that had happened so far. I almost wished we were back in Macon, facing the soldiers with their guns pointed at us. At least we could see all around and had a possibility of escaping. But once we passed the steel gate, it was too late. We couldn't back out; not with Hugh's Turtle directly behind ours. I glanced back to see the giant door roll back down as soon as Hugh cleared the entrance.

Complete darkness engulfed us for about five seconds. I bit back a scream when something touched my hand, but I realized it was Luca. I gripped his hand with more force than I intended, and he squeezed back.

Then the whole tunnel lit up in a way that hurt my eyes. We had been under the cover of thick clouds for days now, and the light was as if the sun was suddenly shining at full power. The vehicle leading us was driving up a ramp to the next floor.

"Silas." Hugh's voice came over our radio.

"Yeah. Just stop. Let's get out and talk."

We climbed out of the Turtles, sniffing the air like we were trying to decide if it was safe to breathe. I wanted to laugh and ask if anyone else had grown up on old sci-fi shows and movies, where the characters had helmets on every time they stepped into unknown terrain. I had been in parking garages before, even big ones in Denver. But this one so deep into the hurricane was so unexpected that it felt like we had landed on a different planet.

Luca had his gun drawn. Silas stepped over to him. "Put that away. Now. Do not let them see it."

Luca pressed his lips together. "Why?"

"Because it's not time for that. And if they have anything bigger than we do, I don't want them dragging it out."

Luca stared at Silas, then unzipped his rain jumpsuit and tucked the gun into the waist of his pants. I kind of was on Team Luca. His gun would be difficult to reach if it were hidden behind so many layers and zippers.

Our team huddled together between the two Turtles.

"Why didn't we follow them?" Jack asked, his eyes on the top of the ramp where our rescue vehicle had disappeared.

"For one thing, we have no idea if the Turtles can fit or turn up there. I'd rather not get trapped. If we need to, we can back out of here."

Ginger was tapping on her tech pad. "They must have fortified this building somehow. I'm having a hard time getting the signal to connect to the satellite."

"Oy! You need the Wi-Fi password?"

We jumped at the sound of the shout. A man stood at the top of the ramp.

"Yes, please," Ginger called back.

"Well, come on up! There's plenty of room up here for your trucks. Are those trucks?"

We all looked at Silas. He turned his back to the men. "Let's walk up there. I still want to leave the Turtles here. Hugh, lock yours down."

Hugh nodded and he and Silas each pressed a few buttons on their hand devices. The Turtles powered down, and the door handles disappeared into the sides of the vehicle.

Silas lead the way up the ramp, and Hugh brought up the rear.

"Whoa, big group!" The man grinned. "How the heck did all of you make it down here?"

Silas stopped at the top. "I'm sorry, I didn't catch your name."

The man laughed. "That's because I didn't give you my name. Since you are in our home, I only feel it's right for you all to introduce yourselves and state your intentions."

Silas eyed him for a moment. "I'm Silas."

The man stuck out his hand. "Nice to meet you, Silas. I'm Atticus. You are welcome here." Silas shook his hand, and Atticus looked at the rest of us. "You all will also be welcome here as soon as you properly introduce yourselves as well."

Silas looked at us and shrugged. "This is Ginger, Hugh, Miri, Jack, Luca, and—"

"Lyla," I said. "I'm Lyla."

To the credit of our group, no one reacted to me jumping in with a fake name. Something in me whispered I shouldn't reveal my real identity. Especially since we did not know who these people were, or how far Chip's influence reached into the hurricane.

Atticus smiled. "It's nice to meet you, Lyla. And the rest of your group. Are you sure you don't want to pull your trucks up here? As you can see, we have plenty of space."

He was right. The second level looked like a typical garage. There were only four other vehicles parked in the space that looked like over a hundred vehicles could fit. This parking garage had clearly been built back before Goliath, but someone had fortified it at some point by covering the openings with massive sheets of metal and thick steel beams.

Silas smiled. "We're okay leaving our trucks where they are."

Atticus narrowed his eyes a bit, but kept the smile on his face. "I guess I should just come out and say that either you need to move your trucks up here, or you need to leave. You can't block our entrance. For safety reasons. Like, what if we need to evacuate?"

Jack's mouth dropped open. "Y'all evacuate out into that storm?"

Atticus shrugged. "If we need to."

Silas and Hugh glanced at each other. "Okay. We could at least get the Turtles turned around and facing in the right direction," Silas said.

Atticus let out a burst of laughter. "Turtles? Is that what you call them? How about that? They kind of do look like turtles."

Jack grinned. "They're slow like turtles, too. But because they are wide and low to the ground, they're safe out there in the wind."

Silas glared at Jack. "And if you have any more questions about them, please ask myself or Hugh."

Jack's cheeks stained pink, and he stepped closer to Miri, as if she could stop him from giving more information than he was supposed to.

The rest of our group moved to the side while Silas and Hugh pulled the Turtles up into the cavernous room.

"So, where're y'all from?" Atticus asked.

We gave each other side glances.

Luca cleared his throat. "Well, we're not from around here."

Atticus laughed hard at that. "Obviously."

Ginger stepped forward with her tech pad. "I'm a meteorologist. We came from Murfreesboro, Tennessee."

"Oh, gosh, y'all are far from home. And you made it all the way here? That's nuts." Atticus looked impressed.

Ginger pulled up an image of Goliath's radar. "Right now, Goliath is a category three, instead of the category five that it usually is. We thought we might come in and get some readings."

Atticus peered at her tech pad. "Whoa. That's what it looks like?"

Ginger nodded and zoomed the image out further. "Yeah, I'm sure this looks like what you've been seeing, but I promise it's different right now. We want to study why."

Atticus shook his head. "We don't have anything that shows us anything like that. We just peek out the door to see if it's still raining, and it always is."

Hugh and Silas pulled the Turtles up into the garage and repositioned them until they were pointing at the ramp. I was glad they did it; this felt like we had a quick way to leave if we needed to.

Atticus seemed mesmerized by the sight of the Turtles. "I've never seen anything like those. We've just had those all these years." He pointed over his shoulder at the ancient-looking humvees. "And, to be honest, we don't have a lot of gas left."

"Gas?" Miri asked. "You mean those use gas?"

Atticus tilted his head. "Yeah. You know, to make them go? How much gas do your Turtles need?"

Hugh pointed at the turbines on the sides. "Those convert wind into the power the Turtles need."

Atticus's mouth dropped open. "So, no gas at all?"

Miri shook her head. "No vehicles have used gas in, like, thirty years."

Atticus rubbed the back of his neck. "Man, I can't wait for Beckett to hear this. He's never gonna believe it."

"How long have you been in here?"

Atticus opened his mouth, then shut it and thought for a minute. "We've been here the whole time. I was born here."

Our group was silent as we stared at him. Hugh finally spoke. "What do you mean the whole time?"

Atticus turned and headed toward the end of the garage, where another ramp lead up. "Come on. I'll show you."

Luca stood still. "Is this a good idea? Leaving the Turtles?"

Silas twisted his mouth. "I think it's fine. They can't access them. And I'm not sure they would even know how to drive them, if all they've ever driven are gas-powered vehicles. Let's just go. But stay together and be ready to get back here if I say to."

We followed Atticus up the second ramp, and then we stopped short. The third level looked like a giant, open-aired street market. There were booths set up in a pattern that looked like streets, and people bustled all over, making transactions.

Jack clutched my arm. "I smell grilled chicken."

My stomach cramped with hunger. The oatmeal meal pod I had eaten hours ago wasn't sticking with me anymore.

"Welcome to Town Center. That's what we call it, anyway. Most people live a couple of levels above us. That's where the school is, too. But here is where people get what they need."

"And you've been here since the start of Hurricane Goliath?" Ginger asked.

Atticus nodded. "Come on. You'll want to meet Deacon. He's the last of the original residents. He can tell you the whole story. I mean, I learned about our town's history in school, but I was never good at presentations."

He took off toward the ramp that lead up once again, and we practically had to run to keep up with him. People stopped and stared at us as we passed. I wanted to stop and stare at them, too. They wore clothes that were popular fifty years ago, things like jeans and fitted shirts. No one wore denim anymore. It wasn't as comfortable as the softer fabric of athletic pants. Fitted shirts went out of style when my mom was a teen.

Of course, who was I to talk. I wore a shapeless rain jumpsuit that was big enough to go over the clothes I had underneath.

Two little girls stood next to the entrance to the ramp, whispering and giggling as we approached. I smiled and gave a wave, which sent them into another fit of giggles.

Atticus stopped in front of the girls and put his hands on his hips. "Nova and Brynn, what are you doing out here?"

The taller girl bit her lip. "We wanted to see the rain people."

"And how did you know about the rain people?"

"Wilder said they were coming. He said his dad went outside, and that means the rain people would come inside."

"And Brynn *always* gets to see them, so I wanted to come with her," the other girl chimed in.

I glanced at Luca. He had narrowed his eyes and was playing with the zipper of his jumpsuit.

Miri stepped up next to Atticus and bent over so she was eye level with the girls. "So, do we look like what you thought?"

Nova giggled. "No way. I thought you'd be wet!"

Miri laughed. "Are the rain people usually wet?"

Atticus cleared his throat. "Girls, go home. You're not supposed to be in the market at this time of day, and you know that. If you go home right now, I won't tell your mom."

The girls' eyes widened, and they scampered up the ramp. Atticus turned back to our group with a smile. "Sorry about that. I'm sure you don't appreciate being treated like livestock."

Silas shrugged. "So, how often do 'rain people' come here, anyway?"

For the first time, Atticus looked uncomfortable. "Well, um, sometimes. Look, if you come with me, our mayor will fill you in." He turned and hurried up the ramp, leaving us to follow.

We hesitated for a minute, then Silas took off after him. Clearly, the answers were on the upper level.

I grabbed Luca's arm. "Is it wise to go so far from the Turtles?"

Luca set his mouth. "I don't know. I guess Silas thinks it's okay. The Turtles are locked down, so I'm not worried about anyone stealing them. But I don't like this either. And I really don't like the risks Silas is taking."

Silas and Atticus were almost at the top of the ramp. I sighed. "I guess I'd rather all stay together. Don't you think? I mean, getting separated from you and your dad in Nashville was the worst thing, because I had no idea how I was going to find you again."

Luca gripped my hand. "You and I are staying together. I promise."

His warm hand on mine settled my racing heart down a notch. "Okay, then. I guess I do want to hear what's up with these people. This is like an entire city."

He nodded, then started up the ramp without letting go of my hand. I matched my pace with him to catch up with the group. The only way to find out if this was a bad idea or not was to keep moving forward.

Chapter 14

"Atticus Bruto, are you kidding me?"

Atticus stopped short and we all almost slammed into each other like an old-timey slapstick video. A petite, stocky woman with her hair piled on top of her head stood in our way with her hands on her hips.

"Hi, Babe! Friends, this is my wife, Sirena. Sirena, meet, uh, Silas, Ginger, um, Maryann, was it?" Atticus cringed as he looked at our faces.

Miri rolled her eyes. "I can see how important it was that we tell you our names, seeing as how you don't remember them now. I'm *Miri*."

Sirena laughed and looped her arm through Atticus'. "Sorry about my husband. His short-term memory is not so good. Babe, did you even give them a tour?"

Atticus shook his head. "No, I was taking them to see Deacon and Murphy."

Sirena rolled her eyes. "I bet ya'll have a million questions. People always do when they stumble on our community. I can answer some, but Atticus is right. Murphy's the best one to talk to. He's our mayor."

Ginger stepped forward. "Can you at least tell us where we are? My GPS glitched, and now I don't trust it."

Sirena raised her eyebrows. "You're in Ousley. No one told you that? Where are you supposed to be?"

Ginger checked her tech pad. "Not in Ousley, that's for sure. That's about eight miles in the opposite direction."

"Ya'll were headed for Valdosta?" Sirena asked.

Silas nodded. "We heard there was a shelter there."

Sirena folded her arms. "I'm not sure, but come with me for a tour while Atticus gets Murphy. How does that sound?"

Ginger tucked her pad back into the shoulder bag she kept. "Yes, that sounds great. We've already seen your market."

Sirena smiled. "Well, this level is farming and hydroponics. We have chickens, goats, rabbits, and most veggies that you want." She took us around the corner and the smell of chicken poop hit us immediately. On one side were all the animals, and hydroponic stations filled the other side. People milled around, tending the animals or the plants.

My mouth dropped open. "How do you power all these lights?"

"Oh, we harvest the wind power from up top. Lord knows we've got plenty of wind to keep the place going. We all live on the next level. Come on up."

Sirena took off up the ramp as fast as Atticus had. She took large steps for someone so short.

"How many people live here?" Ginger asked as she tried to keep up. Hurrying up the ramps was making us all out of breath.

"Well, Link and Lorelai had their second sweet baby just last month, which means we're now at one hundred and two." Sirena looked proud. "Lorelai is my daughter, so I'm a grammy again."

My mouth dropped open. "You don't look old enough to be a grandma."

She laughed. "Well, I *am* forty-two. I had Lorelai at twenty, and she's followin' suit. No reason to wait to have babies here."

"How many families are here?" Hugh asked.

"Hmm. I think we started with ten families. That was about fifty people back when Goliath came." She stopped at the entrance of the level. There were five ancient-looking campers on each wall, and dozens of tents spread out toward the center from there. It looked well-organized, with each tent in a straight line. I half-expected to see a grid painted on the floor, with everyone staying inside their own square. "Well, here's our home camp. It was put on this level because our founders were sure that Goliath was going to cause a flood the size of the one back in Noah's day. This building is our ark. But we guess the wind blows most of the water away, because the flood never came."

"Oh my word, I'm such an idiot." Ginger smacked her head. "That was the one thing I could never figure out. Historically, slow-moving hurricanes produced up to fifteen inches of rain a day, so in Goliath's case, this entire area should have been completely under water by the third day. But there isn't that much rain, is there? It's the wind that's the problem."

Sirena nodded. "Water can get scarce around here. They expected we'd be swimming in it, but we needed to build a collection system. Sometimes we get more water than others, so we've had to learn how to store it, for when the storm decides to dry up for a while. That may have happened once or twice when I was little, but I don't remember that kind of stuff. What I do remember is how my mom made me take care of the chickens when my best friend got to work with the goats. Ooo, I was so mad at her for that."

Sirena was walking while talking, and lead us to the center of the level, where chairs and various boxes sat around a ring of bricks. "The founders had a great idea to have this fire pit in the middle of camp, but they quickly realized that fire in an enclosed space wasn't such a bright idea." She laughed as if that was the town's inside joke. "But the ring is still a good place to gather. Wait here. Atticus and Murphy should be here any minute. Murphy's office is right over there. And Deacon might be awake. If he is, he'll join you too."

Sirena trotted off, finally leaving our group alone. We huddled together.

"Well?" Hugh asked, looking at Silas.

Silas shrugged. "Ginger, have you been able to calibrate the GPS?"

Ginger tapped on the tech pad. "Almost. It helped that Sirena told us we're in Ousley. That means we *did* end up heading west for almost eight miles. And our GPS said we were headed south."

"How did it malfunction like that?" Jack asked.

"You're asking the wrong question," Luca said. "The real question is, who is sabotaging us?"

The group went silent for a moment.

"Are you trying to accuse someone of something, son?" Silas finally asked.

Luca stared him down. "You tell me. First, the military just happens to find us at an unscheduled stop. And Dad gets killed. Now here we are, eight miles in the wrong direction when the whole time our tech was telling us we were on track."

Miri rubbed the back of her neck. "Luca, come on. We know each other. We've been on dozens of missions together."

Her eyes shot to me. My stomach sank. "Oh, do you mean me? Because this is only my second mission?"

Miri shrugged.

Heat flared in my belly. "Why would I sabotage this mission? I'm looking for my *dad*. Which is way more important than whatever you guys are doing. Yeah, getting answers and exposing USHA will make you heroes, but this is my *family* I'm talking about."

Luca stepped in between Miri and me. "We're not accusing Ashlyn."

Miri folded her arms. "Who are you accusing, Denzio? Because clearly you have someone in mind."

Luca set his mouth. "I'm just saying."

Silas held up his hand. "You're right. Things have gone wrong in weird ways that make it seem like someone is on to us. I just don't know who. I really don't."

"Then how did you know about the shelter in Macon?" Luca asked.

That was where all our problems seemed to start. Since Silas was the only one privy to that shelter, it was logical that he might still be holding back details from us.

Silas sighed. "I told you. Matteo. I have a full map of all the shelters he knows about. I'll show you when I can, okay? Not here."

"Hush now, here they come," Ginger hissed.

Atticus and another man walked up to our group. "See, here they are! Gang, this is Murphy Broadman, our town mayor."

Murphy was tall and thin, and his pants were too short. He held out his hand to Silas. "It's nice to meet you folks. We welcome all who seek respite."

Silas shook his hand. "Well, we're not exactly seeking respite. We're on our way to a shelter in Valdosta, but somehow got off course. Tell me, how did you find us? Do you patrol the area?"

"Yeah, how often do you rescue people from the storm?" Hugh asked. "Because those little girls we saw made it seem like 'rain people' come through here on a regular basis."

Murphy smiled and gestured to the seats around the ring. "Sit. I'll explain everything."

Silas folded his arms. "I need to tell you we are on a time crunch here. We have to get to Valdosta today."

"Preferably in the next few hours," Ginger added. "We don't like to travel in the storm in the dark. And the clouds make the daylight way more limited than normal."

Murphy's smile left his eyes, but his lips remained in the curved-upward position. "Well, we can talk about that. I'm sure you're curious about us."

I really was. So I sat on the nearest bench, and Luca sat next to me. The rest of the group sat, too, but with much less enthusiasm.

Murphy remained standing. "First, our town's history. Our founders knew Goliath was going to be different from any other hurricane, so when the government ordered everyone to evacuate on penalty of fine and imprisonment, they came here. The government was checking houses, but they didn't check this structure."

Ginger leaned forward. "What made them believe Goliath would be different?"

Murphy held up his hand. "That's a long story that you folks might not have time for. The point is, this town is ours and we weren't going to let anyone force us out. Now, let's do a little quid pro quo. Why are you headed to Valdosta?"

"We're studying the storm," Ginger said quickly. "Goliath is a Category Three right now. This happens every ten years, and we want to figure out why."

Murphy narrowed his eyes. "Meteorologists? This deep?"

Ginger shrugged. "I mean, we can only get so much data from satellites."

"You realize it's illegal to be here, don't you? Does the government know you're here?"

Silas shook his head and smiled. "This trip is, ah, unsanctioned. But we're scientists. How could we resist?"

Murphy folded his arms. "We know about the shelter in Valdosta. The government built it about two years before Goliath hit. So how can I be sure that you're not *with* the government, here to shut us down?"

Miri stood up. "We just told you; we were headed there, not here. We stole the information about the shelters, okay? We had no idea you even existed. I mean, we could have been talking about you weird Hurricane People for years if we had known."

Murphy studied Miri with her fists clenched and her face turning red. Then he laughed. "Okay. Anyone who is willing to defy the mighty government of the United States is friends of ours, for sure."

Ginger pulled out her tech pad. "We just need to calibrate our GPS, because somehow we got blown off course. Obviously, that's a real concern of ours."

Murphy nodded. "Come to my office. I've got a hard link to the satellite we've used for years. We've never had a problem with it."

Ginger glanced at Silas, and he made eye contact with Hugh and nodded. Ginger and Hugh got up and followed Murphy away from the circle.

A spry old man trotted up to our group and plopped down on the chair that Ginger had just left.

Atticus grinned. "Gramps! Everyone, this is Deacon, my grandpa. He's the last survivor of the Founders."

Deacon looked at each of our faces for a few seconds, then smiled. "Welcome, folks. It's been a long time since we've had visitors."

The wheels in my head began to turn. "But you *have* had visitors before?"

Deacon turned his gaze to me. "Yes. Only a handful in the last fifty years. But we certainly have. Not for a couple of years now, though. This is usually how it goes. Just when I'm sure we're finally good and forgotten about, someone shows up on our doorstep."

My heart pounded. "Do you remember their names?"

Deacon looked up as he thought. "Let's see. There were two fellas about three years ago. Of course, one stayed and one left. Then there was the one guy four years before that.

I'm surprised that the guy made it. He said he had been wandering the storm for a couple of years, hunkering down where ever he could."

Atticus rubbed his chin. "Oh yeah, I remember that guy. We all thought he was part fish or something, swimming around in the storm. But he only stayed here for a night. He said he was headed to the eye. Can you believe that? Why would anyone want to go to the eye? You might as well say that you're walking into the business end of a turbine."

I grabbed Luca's hand. "But what was his name?"

"Something biblical," Deacon said. My heart felt like it was going to come out of my chest. "Matthew, like the disciple."

"No, Gramps. That was Matteo," Atticus said. We all gasped, and Atticus looked surprised. "You guys know a Matteo?"

Silas nodded. "Yeah, we do."

Atticus studied Silas's face. "You kind of remind me of him. So you must know Reuben." He laughed at the look on our faces. "I guess you do. I don't think he's here right now, though. He goes on scavenging missions for us. We do great with what we have, but we can always use something new here."

Things fell into place. Reuben had been the one leading us in the storm. Reuben had spent a lot of time with Ginger and her tech at the shelter last night.

"Anyway, we haven't seen Matteo in a long time. He didn't want to stay."

I couldn't let myself get distracted by news about Reuben. "But what about the other guy? Did you say he was here six years ago? Four years before Matteo?"

Deacon nodded. "Seven years. My mind is still sharp, little lady. His name was biblical, too. And almost fitting, since he was walking around in a storm. You would think his name was Noah, but it was the other one."

I bit my lip, afraid that if I gave him my dad's name, then he might not remember correctly. It would just be me putting an idea in his head.

"Oh, Jonah!" Atticus exclaimed. "Yeah, I remember him."

My breath caught and my vision faded.

CHAPTER 15

I OPENED MY EYES. I was on my back, and Luca was bent over me, stroking my face. Was he staring at my lips? I smiled until I saw Miri near his shoulder. Suddenly, I was aware that everyone was standing over us, staring down at me. Jack was holding my legs up in the air at a forty-five degree angle.

I tried to sit up, but Luca put his hands on my shoulders. "No, stay where you are. Don't get up too fast."

I pushed him away. "I'm fine. Sorry. I don't know what happened." That was a lie. I knew what happened. I solidified everyone's opinion that I was a useless piece of deadweight on this mission. I was a soft, weak little girl who couldn't handle shocking news.

I decided to lay there for a minute. I was furious with myself. There was no reason to faint about the news that Dad had been here. Clues like this were the exact reason I had lied to my family and ditched my best friend, so why was I so surprised that we actually came across one?

I squeezed my eyes shut, and a tear leaked out of my eye.

"Ash?" Luca's concerned voice filled my ears.

"Can you make everyone go away? I need a minute," I whispered. I kept my eyes shut, but Luca must have heard me because Jack lowered my legs onto the floor and I heard footsteps retreat.

I took a deep breath and opened my eyes. Luca sat next to me, his arms wrapped around his knees. I let out a laugh. "Sorry."

He gave a soft grin. "Don't be. It's been a weird day."

I pushed myself into a sitting position, and it took a minute for my equilibrium to come back. "I'm ready to go. Can we go? I mean, Dad was here. It's proof of life. I understand it's seven years old, but we have to keep moving."

Luca nodded. "We're just waiting for Ginger and Hugh to come back."

People had come out of their tents and RVs, blocking our view of Murphy's office. My heart sank, and suddenly I felt trapped. "Are they okay in there?"

Luca stood and held out his hand. I grabbed it and slowly stood up. Atticus began a slow clap, and some of the crowd clapped too. I stopped myself from rolling my eyes. It felt like I was back in the cafeteria at school, when someone tripped and spilled their food, and everyone treated them like they were the entertainment for that day's meal.

"YOU."

We all jumped at the sound of Silas' bellow. He took off running toward the back corner of the camp, people jumping out of his way. I finally glimpsed Reuben, trying to run backwards with his hands up.

"Hey, man! Easy!" Reuben turned and darted around an RV. Silas chased him, and Luca ran to the other side. Sure enough, Reuben flew around the corner at top speed, but Luca was ready. He braced himself and caught Reuben by the arm. Reuben covered his head with his other arm, as if Luca was going to punch him. And for a minute, I thought he might.

Silas grabbed Reuben's other arm and together, he and Luca dragged Reuben back to the ring.

"Okay, okay! I can walk on my own," Reuben said.

Silas shoved him down on a chair and stood over him. "Talk."

"Uh, glad you guys made it! Sorry for losing you back there. I didn't mean to. I bet you were scared. It's nuts when you're driving out there in the windy rain. You gotta know these roads like the back of your hand if you want a prayer of making it anywhere alive." Reuben chattered on the way he did when Luca and Silas had him at gunpoint back at the shelter in Tifton.

"Oh, you're sorry for losing us? Was that your plan all along?" Silas growled.

"No way! Of course not! But I was getting real low on gas and I knew my buddy Atticus would come get you. So I sent you help. It worked, right? You're here? Safe?"

Miri bent over and put her face about two inches from Reuben's. "You *lied* to us."

Reuben shrunk back. "Not really! Well, kind of. But this place is way better than the shelter in Valdosta. I promise. That place is a dump. You can get fresh food here. And more bread. And jam. You liked that, right? But I knew you guys wouldn't want to come here because it's a teeny bit out of your way."

Silas folded his arms. "This doesn't make sense. You said you were with Matteo. Was that true? So where is he?"

Reuben rubbed the back of his neck. "Ah, right now he might be at the shelter in Gainesville. Or maybe Lake City. I don't know. He's somewhere in Florida. But he's waiting for you. I know that."

"But how?"

"I did meet Matteo in Nashville. And I came with him into Goliath to explore the network of shelters. Then once, a few years ago, we got off course and found this place. And this place is awesome! There's no government telling you what to do and everyone is so nice. And I met my wife here. Minka! Come here!"

A woman stepped out from behind the crowd of lookie-loos. She looked to be about my age. Or at least no older than Mella. She had her arms folded across her chest and her lips were in a tight smile as she stepped forward.

"See? This is Minka, my wife. We got married last year."

"Congratulations," Silas said dryly. "Keep talking. Give us actual information."

Reuben licked his lips. "Okay, so Matteo and I found this place, and I fell in love with Minka. And Murphy said we could stay, but Matteo was all about the mission. So he said that this could be my home base, and I would just meet him from time to time to help him out. That's how he told me you were coming. I met up with him in Lake City two weeks ago, and he told me when he thought you would be in Tifton. He asked me to set you up with the good stuff, like the firewood. But you were late, remember? And then I said I would lead you, which I did."

"But what did you do to our tech?" I asked. "Ginger's GPS glitched. Was that you?"

Reuben hunched his shoulders and stared at his feet. "Uh, yeah. I added the signal for this place, which means your tech pad linked as soon as we were in Troupville. I mean, I thought you should come here, but you wouldn't if I told you about it, so I thought if I led you here, then you'd see how great this place is. And then we'd give you good food and you could help us out, too. Because that's how the world goes around, right? People helping each other?"

Silas narrowed his eyes and took a step toward Reuben. "What do you mean, help you out?"

Reuben looked around the crowd, as if someone there was going to help him. "Well, you've got those big Turtles full of equipment. I mean, some of that is extra, right? Like, just in case? Well, I thought maybe you could leave some of it here. And we'd give you good food. That's a good trade off, right?"

Silas looked at the rest of us. "Okay. Time to go."

Jack, Miri, and I stood up, and Atticus jumped into the middle of our group. "Now hold on. No need to rush out."

Silas glared at him. "Please get Ginger and Hugh. We're ready to leave."

"But, wait a minute—"

Silas pulled out his gun and pointed it at Atticus. "I do mean now."

The crowd gasped and backed away. Luca unzipped his jumpsuit and pulled out his gun, too.

"Luca, have Reuben take you to Murphy's office and tell Ginger and Hugh it's time to go."

Reuben eyed Luca's gun, then jumped up and scampered in the direction that Ginger and Hugh and gone, with Luca close behind.

Atticus cleared his throat. "Hey, this was all just a big misunderstanding. And there's no need for that. It's a gun, right? We don't use guns here. We've never had them."

"Well, we did when we started," Deacon said. I jumped. I had forgotten that he was there. He had been sitting in his chair in the ring, watching everything unfold. "Of course, no one brought enough ammo. Atticus is right, we've never needed it. But with the government knocking on our door every month, it's about time for us to restock."

An icy chill ran down my spine. "Every month?"

Deacon nodded. "I don't know why they're bothering us again. In fact, they were here a few days ago."

Silas glared at him. "I thought you said you hadn't had visitors in a few years."

Deacon chuckled. "Oh, they're not visitors. There's nothing neighborly about when they stop by. Mostly they leave us alone, but when they were here they about tore the place apart looking for something. As if we took it."

Jack looked confused. "What were they looking for?"

Minka stepped forward. "Not what. Who."

My heartbeat quickened. "Who?"

She nodded. "Some girl. Ashley?"

Deacon slapped his leg. "Oh, that's right. Booker. Like that fellow who stopped by seven years ago. I remember, because we don't get very many visitors, and it couldn't have been a coincidence that they were looking for someone with the same last name. But I told them that no girl by that name was here. And they didn't ask about any fellow by that name, so I didn't think they needed to have that information."

Luca and Reuben joined our group with Ginger, Hugh, and a man who was not Murphy. Silas pointed his gun at the new guy.

"And who are you?"

The man put his hands up. "Whoa! Please put that down. I'm Wayland, Murphy's brother. He's an idiot."

Silas scowled. "Your brother, the mayor, is an idiot?"

Wayland nodded and looked at the crowd. "This is what I've been talking about, everyone! It's time to recall Murphy. Look what he did; he let Reuben bring armed people into our peaceful town."

The crowd murmured and shifted. "Did you know they had guns, Reuben?" someone shouted.

Reuben held up his hands. "Yeah. But it was Matteo's brother! I was sure he wouldn't hurt anyone. At least, if we didn't hurt him."

Wayland glared at Reuben. "And what happened to your plan about just dealing with the supply convoys? Do these people look like a supply convoy?"

Reuben ducked his head. "No, but they do have supplies! Have you seen their vehicles? They are straight out of the future, man. Sci-fi. They've got stuff that can keep our place going for another few years."

Silas nodded to the rest of us, and we all grouped behind him. "This is how I see it. We didn't take anything from you guys. Not even a bite of food. So we don't owe you anything. So we're going to go, okay?"

Murphy came rushing into the group. "No, wait! Please. You have to help us. Reuben said you have first aid kits. At least give us those."

Wayland shook his head. "We don't need them, Murph. And we don't hijack people."

Half of the crowd nodded and cheered.

"But they've got some medicine we don't have, and that the supply convoy never seems to have. I mean, you guys are mobile, right? You can get whatever you need from one of your other stops. Or you can go back out from the storm. Our vehicles don't have the range to go far, and we're running low on gas. So we have to get the supplies we need, whatever it takes." Murphy climbed on a chair. "This is our town's legacy. Helping each other. And it's our job to teach whoever we come in contact with how to share."

The other half of the crowd seemed to be on Team Murphy. My heart sank.

Silas cocked his gun and fired a shot into a hay bale near the ring. The crowd cried out and jumped back.

"I'm sorry that you guys are missing some things. But we need what we have. And we're leaving. And anyone who tries to stop us will find themselves like that hay bale. And based on what I just heard, I'm not sure you have what you need to treat a gunshot wound here." Silas nodded at us, and we backed away, toward the ramp that would lead us back down to the Turtles.

Wayland scowled. "Yes, go. I promise no one will stop you. Town meeting, right now, everyone! We have some issues to work out."

Silas nodded at us one more time, and we hurried back down the ramp into the hydroponics farm. Silas ran backward, his gun trained on the ramp in case anyone tried to follow us down. The workers on the farm stood frozen as we raced by, unaccustomed to seeing guns.

The market was still busy, and no one paid any attention as we ran through. Silas must have finally felt comfortable because he turned and ran face forward with the rest of us down the final ramp to the parking garage.

I breathed a sigh of relief when I reached the garage to see that our Turtles were still sitting there.

"Wait!"

Silas and Luca immediately pulled out their guns and trained them on the voice behind us. Minka took slow steps toward us with her hands raised.

"Anyone with you?" Silas barked.

Minka shook her head and kept her eyes on the floor. "I just need to say something to that girl."

Silas lowered his weapon, and Luca followed suit. "Which girl?"

Minka peeked up. "Um, Ashley? She's with you, right?"

Luca stepped forward and in front of me. "Why would you think that?"

Her brown eyes filled with tears. "We have satellite internet. I looked up the girl on Murphy's computer after those soldiers were here, because I thought she might be in trouble. And you're her, right?" She looked at me.

I bit my lip and rubbed my hands through my short hair. "My name is Ashlyn. I guess changing my hair didn't work."

She gave a small smile. "No, it looks great. I'm just really good with faces. But I need to talk to you. Maybe, alone? We can just go over there, so your friends can still see you."

My curiosity about what Minka had to say was so strong that I couldn't bring myself to leave. She looked like a timid girl, so following us down here knowing that Silas and Luca had guns must have meant that it was important.

Ginger looked at Silas. "I could use a minute to check our map. I'm pretty sure which direction to go, but it would be better for us to look at it together before splitting up into the Turtles."

Silas grunted. "Okay. Be fast. I want to leave, like now."

Luca folded his arms. "I'll be right here."

I turned to Minka and gave her a smile. "Okay, let's go over there."

CHAPTER 16

I FOLLOWED MINKA TO the other side of the garage. She went way farther than was necessary to get out of earshot of the others. She stopped, looked over my shoulder to make sure no one had followed us, then motioned for me to move closer. I leaned in. She whispered something, but the roaring wind rattling the metal coverings on the wall drowned out her words.

"What?"

"They know where you're going," she said a little louder.

"Who?"

"The military."

I hesitated. I didn't want to give out information, but I needed to find out what she was talking about. "Where do they think we're going?"

Minka's eyes filled with tears and she took a deep breath. "Reuben told them about your schedule for the shelters. He was trying to get them to give us some extra supplies, and he thought that information about you would help. But they didn't give us anything this time. Not even the water purification tablets they carry to make the rain water safe to drink."

My blood ran cold. "How did he know about me?"

Minka wiped her eyes. "Matteo. When Matteo told him about your team coming through, he told Reuben about you and how you were coming to find your dad."

My heart quickened. "Does Reuben know my dad?"

She shook her head. "No, I don't think so. I mean, he knows who Jonah Booker is. But he only talks about working with Matteo. I asked him about it after the military came here last time, and Reuben said he's never met him. They believe he went into the eye, but they've never established communications in there. And since no one has ever come out of the eye, they've never tried to go in."

I bit my lip. "Okay. Well, I need to tell my team this."

She grabbed my arm. "But you can't. It's not safe."

"Why? I mean, I have to tell them. We're all travelling together."

She shook her head. "Silas told Reuben and Matteo everything. He's the one who tells them about the military supply convoys."

"So? I know Silas is working with Matteo."

Frustration crossed Minka's face. "Silas is the one giving the military information."

My mouth dropped open. "Are you sure?"

"Yes, Reuben tells me everything. Because he's my husband. And he's a nice guy and sometimes the lying he has to do gets to him. It really bothered him that he had to lie to you guys to get you here, and he usually feels better after he tells me."

I shifted my weight and tried to process. On one hand, what she was saying made zero sense. What would Silas gain by being a double agent? But he did take us to a shelter that Tyler didn't know about, and the military just happened to show up at a crazy early hour in the morning, before we left.

I swallowed hard. "Did Reuben say anything else? Like what Matteo and Silas' actual plans are? Because it was my understanding that our plan was to get to the eye and back out again, so that the Storm Chasers would have solid proof about what is going on in there."

Minka sighed. "All I know is that Reuben is excited that Silas finally brought a team in here because he says it's going to make us rich. We like to talk about moving away from here, like out into good weather. He keeps talking about Montana, where there are mountains, and sunshine, and snow."

"How is this going to make you rich?"

Minka shrugged again. "I just thought I should tell you, because I know you want to find your dad. And I think it's really brave that you came into Goliath for that."

I fingered the ends of my short hair. "Well, thanks. I guess I'm stuck, though. I'll try to be careful."

"Or you could go the other way to the eye."

I threw up my hands. "There's another way? And you're just now mentioning it?"

Minka gave a bashful smile. "Sorry. Yeah, there are smaller shelters you could go to. Reuben found them. He took me to one on our honeymoon. It was nice to be in a little place by ourselves. There's no place to be alone here, not really."

"And the military doesn't know about these?"

"I don't think so. They're too small for the convoys, so they would have never considered them. Reuben said that they were all made by regular people. They're really good shelters, but too small to live in forever. The people who built them had to move on, we guess."

"And there are shelters all the way to the eye?"

She nodded and pulled a piece of paper out of her pocket. "Here are the towns. I bet you could find them easy enough. I've only been out of this garage once, but I know there aren't any other buildings anywhere, except for these concrete ones."

I slipped the list in the pocket of my pants under my rain jumpsuit and hoped it would stay dry. "Thank you. So much. I wish I could repay you somehow."

She smiled. "I just wanted to make up for Reuben freaking you guys out. He really is a good guy."

"Booker, we gotta go," Silas boomed out across the garage.

I looked over my shoulder and gave him a thumbs up. By the time I looked back, Minka had already disappeared up the ramp to the next level. I hustled back to the Turtles. Everyone had already loaded in.

Miri raised her eyebrows as I buckled in. "So? What did she want?"

I tried to keep my movements calm and normal as I settled in. "She wanted to apologize for Reuben. She said he always feels really bad when he lies, and she wanted to tell me what a good guy he is."

Silas grunted as he put the Turtle in gear and moved forward. "Yeah, good guy. Sure. I can't wait to talk to Matteo about him. He was always too trusting."

Luca glanced over his shoulder at me, and I gave him a pointed look. He raised his eyebrows, and I mouthed the word "later." He gave a small nod, then faced forward.

Out of the corner of my eye, I could tell that Miri caught that whole exchange. I inwardly cringed. I didn't want to bring her in on this. But I wasn't sure I'd be able to keep her out of it. I didn't want Silas to be aware of it, so I looked at Miri and nodded at her too. She seemed satisfied and faced forward to watch our journey.

The shelter in Valdosta was less than ten miles away from the parking garage in Ousley. Silas swore several times about being led off course by Reuben, and Miri teased him about his language.

The shelter looked like all the others from the outside, but once we got inside, we realized Reuben was right. This place was a dump. Well, stripped anyway. The people of Ousley must have ransacked this for supplies at some point. There wasn't any furniture of any kind. The only thing left in the space was the black wood-burning stove that they hadn't been able to move. There was no wood to burn.

Silas sighed. "Well, we have air mattresses. But they're in the chests that are buried the deepest in the Turtles."

"Ashlyn and I can get them," Luca said. I tried to keep my face neutral, but I was thrilled he came up with it. That would give us a chance to chat without being overheard in the echoey shelter.

"Yeah, and I'll help," Miri piped in. Darn, I had forgotten about her.

"Me too," Jack said. "Kid power!"

I looked at Luca, and he shrugged. I wasn't prepared for that wrinkle. But I didn't have any reason to keep him from helping.

Silas nodded, then turned to help Ginger and Hugh pull the tech out from the chest we had already brought inside.

The four of us slipped back out the door into the cold carport. At least it was dry out there.

Luca pulled open one of the back doors of the closest Turtle. "Jack, you and Miri check this Turtle. Ashlyn and I will check the other." Miri looked like she wanted to object, but she had no reason to. Pulling out the chests from the Turtles was a two-person job.

We walked to Hugh's Turtle, which had its back edge poking out at the end of the carport. The wind was strong and loud.

"So?" Luca asked without looking at me.

"Minka said that Silas is working with USHA."

Luca paused what he was doing and glanced at me. "And how does she know?"

"Reuben told her. Apparently, he has a lot of guilt about lying and deception, and he absolves himself by confessing everything to her."

Luca pulled out a chest and opened it up. "What else?"

"She said that Reuben told the military convoy that stopped by a few days ago our exact timing for the shelters. He was trying to get them to give the Ousley garage more supplies by giving them information about where I would be, but the convoy didn't give them anything in return."

That made Luca stop. "So, they know we're going to be here?"

I shrugged and nodded. "Yeah. But what can we do about it? I mean, Minka gave me a list of other towns on the way to the eye that have much smaller shelters, but how would we get there?"

Luca slammed the lid on the chest closed and reached for another one. "We'll take a Turtle."

My mouth dropped open. "How? These things move at, like, two miles per hour. It's not like we could outrun anyone."

"We'll leave tonight. At two o'clock."

"Woot! Got 'em!" Jack yelled. He and Miri dragged the chest into the shelter, with Miri looking over her shoulder at us the whole time.

Luca and I put the chest back into the Turtle. "What about Jack and Miri?" I asked.

Luca narrowed his eyes. "We should definitely not tell Jack. He can't keep his mouth shut about anything."

"Miri watches you like a hawk," I said.

A cute half-grin appeared on Luca's face. "Do I hear jealousy, Booker?"

My cheeks heated. "No. I'm just saying, I'm not sure we'll be able to slip past her." He looked over his shoulder. Jack and Miri hadn't returned yet. He turned back to me and leaned in close, the intensity in his eyes causing a butterfly storm in my chest. "You have nothing to worry about."

I panicked. "What are you talking about?"

He reached down and grabbed my hand. "Miri is a good friend. She's like a sister, or a cousin. I've never had any feelings besides friendship for her."

I glanced at our hands. "Luca, what are you doing? What happened to focusing on the mission? And not taking advantage of me after my break up?"

He tightened his grip as a shadow crossed his face. "Life is short."

The butterflies disappeared as my throat closed. I pulled my hand away. "I think it's time for *me* to not take advantage of *you*. You're grieving, Luca. This wouldn't be right."

Longing filled Luca's eyes. "Please, Ashlyn? This is exactly what I need right now. My head is clear. And life really is short. This mission is more dangerous than I thought, and I don't want to waste any time."

My heart broke for him, and I reached for his hand this time. He laced his fingers through mine. This might be a mistake, but he was right. Life *was* short. And if we didn't make it out of this storm, I didn't want any regrets. And I would regret it if I didn't explore this thing with Luca.

"I have a feeling that whatever I choose, I'm going to regret something," I said.

He cocked an eyebrow. "Wouldn't it be better to regret something fun, rather than something that's boring?" He leaned down and pressed his lips to mine.

It was time to admit how badly I wanted him to do it. I reached up with my other hand and ran my fingers through his hair as the kiss deepened. I had been a little afraid that if I ever kissed Luca, then all I would think about was Mason. But that kiss made me forget everything, even Hurricane Goliath.

The kiss only lasted a few seconds before Luca pulled away, his eyes searching mine. He must have liked what he saw, because a shy grin filled his face. My cheeks flamed, and I stepped back. The howl of the wind brought the mission back into focus.

"You're good at that, Booker."

I punched him in the arm. "So, two o'clock?"

He nodded. "I'll get Hugh's com that connects to this Turtle. Let's try to sleep closest to the door."

"How will we wake up without waking everyone else up?"

Miri cleared her throat, and I jumped away from Luca as if I had been burned. How long had she been standing there? Did she see us kiss? "My watch has a silent timer. What time are we getting up?"

Luca calmly gestured with his head as if her walking up on us was perfectly natural, and she stepped in close. I tried to read her face, but she wasn't looking at me. She kept her eyes on Luca. "We need to leave at two. Minka gave Ashlyn a list of towns that have shelters, and we need to get away from Silas."

Miri's eyes narrowed. "And why do you trust Minka, a girl we just met, and who has demonstrated her ability to judge character by marrying Reuben, over Silas?"

Luca folded his arms and his face darkened. "Because Dad didn't trust him. You heard him. Soldiers showed up at our unscheduled stop."

"But you heard Reuben. They stay away from that shelter because it's watched by the military."

He sighed. "Look, we don't have a lot of time to figure this out. We've got to get to the eye by Sunday. So we have three days. And Dad is right. We have to get to the eye to get evidence of what is going on. If someone has the power to create and maintain this storm, then who's to say they won't try to take over some other part of our country?"

I jumped in. "And Reuben told the military convoy about our planned stops. So they know where we're going to be and when. Which means we need to go."

"And if Silas really is somehow acting like a double agent, then we can't risk bringing him in on this plan," Luca said. "What if he gives away our position?"

Miri sighed. "Well, you know I'm with you, Denzio. But I don't like this. I have no idea what Silas could gain by working with them. It doesn't make sense."

I threw my hands up. "None of this makes sense. I mean, we're used to this storm because it's been here our whole lives. But people used to live here, but now it's a wasteland. And history says no hurricane ever lasted more than a day or two."

Miri scowled. "I already said I'm in. But I just want to make sure we're not being idiots by going to shelters we know nothing about."

"We know nothing about these shelters," Luca said. "We're just trusting Silas. So I don't see the difference between going to these and trying to find our own."

Jack bounced up to our group. "Hey guys, we found them."

Luca nodded. "Yeah, we're coming. We were packing back up this Turtle."

Jack bounded back into the shelter, and Miri gave one nod. "Got it. Two."

We headed inside, my stomach in knots. I wanted to get more detailed plans, but there was no time.

I just hoped we'd leave before the military showed up.

CHAPTER 17

We didn't need Miri's watch, because I couldn't sleep. Not even to the soothing white noise coming from the device Ginger kept near her head. I heard every single shift and sigh from the others in the room, fully convinced that no one was actually sleeping, and that they would catch us trying to leave. Every ten minutes, Hugh let out a snort, like he was startling himself awake.

Finally, Miri touched my leg. I slid out from under my sleeping bag, trying to minimize the rustle of the lightweight fabric. No one had seemed to notice that Luca, Miri, and I had gone to bed with our shoes on. I bunched up my sleeping bag, grabbed my pack, and took slow steps toward the door.

Ginger had left one battery-powered lantern on, set at its dimmest setting. It was enough light to help us not step on anyone, but dim enough so that everyone slept. Luca and Miri had stopped at the door with their packs, Luca's hand on the handle. He had a stricken look on his face.

I realized the problem, too. The wind howled outside, but the heavy door to the shelter kept the sound to a very muffled roar. Opening the door would change everything.

Miri, Luca, and I stared at each other, each shrugging our shoulders. Tears filled my eyes. This would not work. We were stuck. And Chip's goons were going to catch up with me and make me go back home. And Chip would marry Mom, and Mom would become an accidental bigamist, and Chip would become President of the United States, and no one would ever learn that the government was keeping the storm going somehow because they made so much money harvesting wind and rain power. The blood rushing in my ears got louder, and I wondered if this was what a panic attack was like.

I almost let out a squeak when someone touched my arm, interrupting the downward spiral of my thoughts. But the loud rushing sound remained. Miri was pointing over at the sleeping adults. Jack was crouched by Ginger's head, his hand on her sound device. I realized he had been gradually increasing the sound on her machine, so the roar of the white noise would match the volume of the wind.

Jack smiled and gave a thumbs up. I pressed my lips together and touched my hands to my lips in a thank-you gesture. He nodded at me, then nodded toward the door with his eyes opened wide. My heart broke a little. He was helping us. Guilt squeezed my stomach at the thought of leaving him behind. He saw my hesitation and mouthed the word "go."

Luca pulled open the door just wide enough for us to squeeze through, then eased it shut once we were outside in the carport. I opened my mouth to speak, but Luca shook his head and pointed at Hugh's Turtle. We hustled to un-link the chains, and I cringed when Miri dropped hers on the concrete floor. We froze for a moment, then all jumped into the Turtle, Luca in the driver's seat, me in the passenger seat, and Miri in the seats behind ours.

Luca pulled out Hugh's pad and hit a button. The Turtle whirred to life, and he backed out of the carport, grunting as the wind hit the back of the Turtle. He gripped the steering wheel tighter and kept moving. The difference in the wind was noticeable.

"Get the Turtle pad," he said. "There are settings we can change to help move the wind panels."

I grabbed the pad and touched the screen. Thankfully, the interface was intuitive. "I had no idea these vehicles were designed this way. I never even saw Silas messing with the settings."

"That should have been another red flag." Luca grunted. "I wish Dad and I had caught all this sooner. A good team trains all members in the basic knowledge of all things. Sure, people can specialize, but there shouldn't just be one or two who know how to use the tech we have."

"That's not fair," Miri said. "We only had a few weeks to prepare. There wasn't time to train everyone."

I glanced back at Miri. It was still so dark outside, and her face was lit by the faint glow of the tech pad she had taken from Ginger. Miri always had a resting angry face, but this time her face looked mad on purpose. "You still think we're wrong about Silas?"

"Yes, I do. And it's not fair to him we're taking off like this."

Luca inched the Turtle forward, the driving sideways rain in the headlights making it almost impossible to see the road. "It's like you said, Day. We didn't have time. There's no time to talk through everything to death. We just have to decide sometimes."

Miri let out a low growl. "You're right. But I can hate it. Now, where are we going?"

I pulled the piece of paper that Minka had given me out of my bra. It was the safest place I could think to keep it. I used the light from the Turtle tech pad to read the handwritten list. "The first town on the list is Traxler."

She tapped on the pad. "That's in Florida. About eighty-five miles from here."

I glanced at my pad. "And we're going five miles an hour right now. So we'll be there in seventeen hours."

"And so Silas and the others will catch up with us in five," Miri said. "Come on, Denzio. Can't you go faster?"

A gust of wind blasted us from the side, as if Goliath wanted to weigh in on our conversation. Luca swore, and I hit a button on the tech pad to adjust the wind panels one more time. "It's pitch black out and raining. If I go any faster, I might run us off the road. My goal is to make it to the eye alive, Miri."

It was the first time I had heard him use her first name, rather than "Day." That alone told me how tense he was. I wanted to reach over and rub his neck to ease the tension, but I didn't want to distract him. I also wasn't comfortable with any signs of physical affection with Miri sitting two feet behind us. I realized that three were better than two on this mission, but I kind of wished she had stayed in the shelter with Jack.

My tech pad told me that Luca had increased our speed to ten miles per hour. "Don't do anything that feels unsafe. Any distance we can get right now is good. And it will lighten when the sun comes up. We can go faster then."

Miri let out an enormous sigh. "She's right, Denzio. Sorry."

We rode in silence for a little while. There wasn't anything to do or say. The burden was on Luca.

"Remember the sun?" I asked. Neither Miri nor Luca replied. "I just remembered it. When I said that it will get lighter when the sun comes up. Minka told me she had never even seen the sun before."

Miri scoffed. "That's crazy."

"It's crazy that there is a whole town inside Goliath. We never even talked about that. So many of those people have never been outside of that garage. It's weird, right?"

Miri let out a laugh. "Yeah. It's like some weird cult. Luca, remember those families that lived in the RV park next to Cherry Creek Reservoir? They had, like, ten RVs at the very back of the lot, as far away from anyone else as possible. Even though it meant they had to walk like a mile to the public showers. Not that they ever used them. The ones who smashed all the pumpkins every October?"

"Oh yeah." Luca's half-grin appeared in the dim light of the dash screen. "And they only wore the colors brown or green, right?"

"That's right! I forgot about that. That one girl who loved you? What was her name? She kept bringing you brown shirts, telling you that your black ones invited evil and that you'd look so much better in brown."

Luca let out a snort. "And I wore only black shirts from then on. I think her name was Allegra."

Miri let out a laugh. "Oh my gosh. That's right. They were all named something musical. Carol, Piper, Harmony."

I tried to smile, but I felt left out. Neither one of them was even trying to give me more information or bring me in on whatever inside jokes they had. I glanced at Luca, who had his eyes on the road and his hands on the wheel still. At least his face looked more relaxed. I tried to relax myself. Anything to ease the tension, right?

I leaned my head back while Luca and Miri chattered on about the weird people they used to know. I didn't want to distract Luca from his driving, and Miri's conversation seemed to help him. I stared out the window at the rain in the headlights. The wind was blowing so hard that the rain almost looked like snow. Somehow I drifted off to sleep, because when I woke up, it was much lighter outside. I sat up with a gasp.

Luca gave me a side glance, the dimpled half-grin on his face. "Nice nap, Booker?"

I looked over my shoulder, trying to wipe the drool off of my mouth without drawing attention to it. Miri was asleep, clutching her tech pad. "Yeah. Sorry."

"Don't be. Remember what Dad said? Sleep when you can, Rookie."

A lump grew in my throat. Had the train ride to Nashville really only been four days ago? It seemed as if it had been years. I studied Luca's face. He was still relaxed and calm. How could he be so chill about his dad being killed a couple of days ago?

"You're staring, Booker."

"Not staring. Wondering how you can be so okay with everything."

Luca stared straight ahead. "I'll deal with it later. I don't have time right now. And this is what Dad wanted, so I can do it."

His tone told me to let it be. I squeezed his shoulder anyway, and he gave me a quick look that sent warm fuzzies through my chest. I glanced again at Miri. Still asleep.

"Where are we?"

He gave a little shrug. "I'm positive we're still on I-75. I haven't made any turns at all. Slow and steady wins the race, right? I can tell you we've gone about twenty-seven miles. I'm picking up the pace now, though. Silas will know we're gone. In fact, I bet they left the shelter an hour ago, and I don't want them catching us."

The Turtle pad told me we were now going about twenty-five miles per hour. That was as fast as Silas had ever gone yesterday. I hoped we had enough distance between us that he couldn't catch up.

"We have sixty-six miles to go to Traxler," Miri said in a sleepy voice. "Sorry, I conked out there. You're on track. Do you need a break?"

Luca shook his head. "No, we can't stop. I'm fine. If we're going twenty-five miles per hour, then we should be there in…"

"About three hours," I finished for him.

He gave a warm smile. "Quick on the math skills, Booker."

I shrugged. "Simple calculations are my super power."

"So is flirting," Miri muttered under her breath.

I looked at her. "Excuse me?"

She opened her eyes wide. "Nothing. I just said you're right."

"Booker, do you have any food?" Luca asked.

"I got it," Miri said. Once again, my stomach clenched. Miri was taking care of Luca, not me. To be fair, all our packs were on the floor next to her. But it seemed like she was butting in. She handed two protein bars over the seat, and I grabbed them. I opened one end and wrapped the bar for easy handling, then held it out for Luca.

"Thanks. Ooo unwrapped and everything. Will you feed it to me, too?"

I rolled my eyes. "In your dreams."

"Definitely."

Miri coughed. "Anyone want water?"

"No thanks," I replied. What I wanted was a bathroom. But there was no time or place for that. Which meant I had to drink as little water as possible.

The next few hours were the same. Luca seemed to relax more the farther we went, but I grew more uneasy as the day went on. Would Silas catch up with us? I should have calmed down once we passed Lake City, since that's where Silas planned to stop next. Once we were past that stop, Silas wouldn't know where we were going, but I couldn't relax.

At last, Miri spoke the words that I had been hoping to hear all day. "Traxler is coming up."

Luca rolled his head from side to side. "So, how do we find the shelter?"

I leaned forward. "Minka said that there's nothing else here. Everything has been blown away. We should be able to find it easy."

"The map shows an exit to the east. Take that and we'll just have to drive around, I guess." Miri tapped on the pad. "Oh, and the radar shows a dark red patch moving toward us. It'll be here in, like, ten minutes. So if we need to find the shelter and get in before that."

I was getting tired of Goliath acting like the stowaway on our road trip. Luca eased the Turtle off the highway, and we all three tried to see through the driving rain. After five minutes of driving east, I started to think that we had made a huge mistake. There was nothing in sight.

I swallowed hard. "Guys. Maybe we should go back to Lake City."

"No. We'll find it." Luca pressed forward.

"There!" Miri leaned over the seat and pointed toward our left. "See that dark shape?"

Any kind of shape was a good sign. Luca aimed the Turtle, and we pulled up to a shelter about a third of the size of any we had stayed in so far. There was no carport on this one. He pulled around the side so that the shelter was blocking some of the wind.

Luca took a deep breath. "Okay. I see a pipe on the side of the shelter we can use to the chain up the Turtle. I guess we'll only take our packs in, since trying to unload anything will get it wet."

Miri was already stuffing things into our packs. "Got it. I've pulled out some meal pods. Ashlyn, hand me that pad and I'll bury it under something so it doesn't get wet."

I froze. "What if we can't get in? What if the door is locked or something?"

Luca gave me an exasperated look. "Didn't you say Minka had been here? How did they get in?"

Miri rolled her eyes as she tightened her rain hood and pulled down her goggles. "I'll go try the door. Hang on."

Before we had a chance to respond, Miri popped open the door and dashed to the shelter without clipping on her harness. The door to the shelter opened, and she pulled it back shut without going inside, and ran back to the Turtle. "We're good! I've got your pack, Luca. Ashlyn, here's yours. Luca, chain the Turtle."

Luca and I finished pulling on our hoods and goggles, and we all moved as quickly as we could out into the wind. The wind was stronger than I had ever felt it and, for one second, I thought that this might be the time that Goliath finally blew me away. But Miri grabbed my arm, and we made it to the door and pushed our way in.

The warmth of the room hit me almost as hard as the wind outside. I pulled up my goggles and stopped short. A man sat at a table in the small room.

"Ashlyn Booker, I presume."

CHAPTER 18

Luca ran into my back, and I almost fell over.

"What are you guys doing?" he asked, as he turned and pushed the door closed. Then he turned and saw the unexpected occupant of the shelter. He jumped in front of Miri and me. "Hey!"

He fumbled with his rain jumpsuit, trying to reach his gun. The man put his hands up.

"Whoa, calm down." He kept his hands up and his movements slow. He looked out of place in Goliath, wearing a simple short-sleeved T-shirt. Tattoos covered his arms. If Trig were here, he'd have plenty to say about so many tattoos on someone who seemed old enough to be our dad. "Sorry to surprise you."

"Who are you?" I asked. "And how did you get here?"

Miri scowled. "Yeah, there are no vehicles out there."

The man gave a small smile, his hands still in the air. "One of my teammates dropped me off, and he's coming back with supplies. But I needed to get here before you did."

Luca got his rain jumpsuit unzipped, and he pulled out his gun.

The man eyed the gun, but remained still. "I'm Matteo."

My mouth dropped open as I caught a glimpse of a dolphin tail peeking out under his sleeve on his bicep. The minute he said his name, I realized how similar he looked to Silas. "You are? You knew my dad?"

Matteo gave a slight nod. "I did. And I would much rather prefer to chat without a gun pointed at me. Can we?"

I looked at Luca, afraid he would prevent me from getting info about Dad. My heart turned over at the look on his face. He was worried about me. His eyes softened and gave a brief nod at me as he put his gun down.

Matteo sighed. "Thank you. I'm sure you have a ton of questions. Settle in, take a seat. Sorry, there's not much seating in these tiny places."

This shelter was about the quarter of the size of the others we had been to. There were two bunks side by side on one wall, just two steps away from the wood-burning stove. A table with four chairs sat in the middle of the room. The far end of the shelter had a walled-off area that I assumed was the bathroom.

Matteo laughed. "Yes, it's a bathroom. I bet you need it, don't you? You've been on the road for, what, six hours?"

Luca frowned. "Eight. And it bothers me that you seem to know so much about what we've been doing."

I held up my hand. "I do have to go. But I don't want to miss anything. So everyone stop talking for a few minutes, okay?"

Matteo grinned, and Luca gave a resigned shrug. I headed to the bathroom, grateful for the walls and door. The door was thin, but at least it was better than the curtain in Macon. I rushed to take care of myself and hurried out into the main room.

Miri and Luca each took their turns while we sat in awkward silence, trying to not listen to the sounds coming from the bathroom. Well, as much silence as the howling winds of Goliath would allow. This shelter's door wasn't as strong as the others. As soon as Luca settled back at the table, he folded his arms. "Talk."

Matteo leaned back in his chair, like we were old friends settling in for a chat. "Silas woke up at about five this morning and found you gone, obviously. He immediately radioed me. I figured if you took off without him, then you wouldn't head to the shelter in Lake City."

My stomach dropped. "But how did you guess we'd come here?"

"He told me about your detour in Ousley, so I guessed you learned about the other shelters from Reuben. So I called him, and he said Minka told you about the small shelters we had found."

Luca frowned. "And did you tell Silas where we were?"

Matteo shook his head. "I told him to stay on course, and I'd find you. Come on, guys, it's not that hard. Of course you'd stay on I-75. You only got a few hours head start on Silas."

Miri sighed and put her head in her hands. "I knew we wouldn't be able to get away from Silas."

Matteo leaned in. "Why are you trying to get away from Silas?"

I looked at Luca and Miri. I struggled to decide whether to trust him or not. On one hand, Matteo had history with Dad. And he was the one feeding Silas the information that got us this far. On the other hand, we still didn't know how the military found us, and if Silas was involved, was his brother involved too?

"We have a mission," Luca said. "And we were no longer sure that Silas supported the mission. And we didn't have time to hash it out, so we ventured on our own."

Matteo studied Luca through narrowed eyes. "That's a cryptic answer."

He shrugged. "Since you're in such tight contact with Silas, it's the best you're going to get."

Matteo sighed. "You overestimate our communication ability in this storm. You know that's part of what your team is doing, right? Setting up com equipment at the shelters to boost the signal? I've been down south, so I'm still stuck with brief messages."

Miri folded her arms. "Well, then there's the fact that your boy Reuben waylaid us to steal our supplies for Ousley."

Matteo rolled his eyes. "Yeah, sorry. I should have known his marriage would cause problems one day. He'll do anything for his wife. You can't blame him for that, can you?"

I frowned. "I can blame him for telling the convoy about when we'd be at each of the next shelters."

A cloud came over Matteo's face. "He did what? Okay, I'm gonna punch him the next time I see him."

"He said he did it because Chip Sinclair sent soldiers after me, and he thought he'd get more supplies from the convoy if he gave them my location.

His nostrils flared. "Chip. That guy has always been a thorn in my side. Your dad always said they were good friends, but I always saw right through him. He was nothing but a slimy opportunist."

I let out a mirthless laugh. "He still is. Have you heard he's dating my mom?"

"What?"

I nodded. "Yeah, he plans to marry her. And run for President of the United States. I guess he needs a wife and kids, because that looks better for a presidential campaign. But I know that Dad's still alive, and he's the only one who can stop him."

Matteo rubbed the back of his neck. "Oh man."

I leaned forward. "Dad *is* still alive, isn't he?" A lump formed in my throat. I felt like I was about to get the answer either way, and suddenly I wasn't sure if I was prepared.

He reached over and placed his hand on my arm. "I haven't seen your dad in ten years. I've seen evidence of his in Goliath, but never caught up with him. The last thing I saw was his name on a log dated three years ago. I believe he is alive, but I don't have proof. I'm sorry."

A tear dripped down my face, and Luca scooted closer to me. He laced his fingers through mine and squeezed. "That's not a no, Booker."

I took a deep breath and wiped my cheeks. "Sorry. I just got my hopes high for a second that you had the answers."

Matteo leaned back. "I still don't understand why you guys left Silas. He is headed for the eye. And there is safety in numbers."

Luca let go of my hand. "Did Silas tell you my dad was killed in Macon?"

Matteo grew still. "No. I'm so sorry to hear that. Like I said, I only get short messages from him, not big updates."

I put my hand on Luca's leg. "Somehow, the military caught up with us. There was a gun fight, and Tyler died along with the three soldiers. Since Silas was the only one with information about the Macon shelter, we aren't sure if he's the one who tipped them off."

Miri nodded. "And Minka told us that Silas is the one who gives you and Reuben information about the supply convoys that come through here. Since the military is after Ashlyn, we had to leave."

It was silent for a few minutes. Matteo seemed to be in deep thought, and a look of exhaustion came over Luca.

Luca stood up and looked at Miri and me. "I need to nap. Are you guys okay?"

I squeezed his hand. "Yes, of course. Don't worry."

Matteo nodded. "I promise I'm not here to hurt anyone. As soon as I got word that Jonah's daughter was missing, I just wanted to find her."

My heart warmed. Deep down, I knew I could trust him. Dad did, back when they worked together. And Matteo came into the storm as soon as he could after Dad went missing. I may not have known what was going on with Silas, but I felt I could trust Matteo with our lives.

Luca leaned down and whispered to me. "Please wake me up if you need me. For anything. I mean it."

I almost forgot that there were other people in the room, and I was about to lean forward to press a kiss to Luca's lips when Miri gave a little cough. My face flamed. "I promise. We'll be fine. We're not going anywhere."

Matteo looked at us. "Mind if I make some hot water? Hot water goes great with meal pods."

Luca nodded and headed for the bunks. He curled on his side and seemed to fall asleep immediately. Matteo stood up for the first time and headed to the stove. He moved a pot that had water in it and shoved a stick of wood in the stove's belly.

"Where did you get dry wood?" Miri asked.

"We have a store house where we take wood to dry out. Which is really hard, as you can imagine. It takes a few years, in fact. But whoever built the shelters you've been going to also created storage sheds that had things like dry wood for these stoves. It took us a few years, but we found those. They weren't on the map."

I snapped my fingers. "That's right. Reuben said you had found a map to the shelters."

Matteo nodded. "I found the map on Chip's computer about a month after your dad went missing. That's when I decided I had to go into Goliath myself to find him. I was so mad that it wasn't something your dad and I had access to. I mean, clearly Chip had information about the shelters when we were planning our mission. But he sent your dad in blind, as if we had no data to go on."

The slow burn of rage I usually felt about Chip started in my chest. "And I thought he had just sabotaged Dad by cutting his supplies in half. But he could have helped."

Matteo sat down while he waited for the water to boil. "Don't worry. Your dad found the shelter in Tifton on his own. He holed up there for a few months before venturing out."

"How do you know?"

Matteo smiled. "He left detailed logs. Jonah has always been an excellent scientist. Very methodical. He always said that leaving data behind was the key to figuring out the storm."

I perched on the edge of my seat. "How did he move around? No one has ever told me."

"He used an electric humvee that had a charger that was powered by wind. He could go about thirty miles at a time, then had to set up the wind charger to recharge the battery. That entire process took about twelve hours."

I shook my head. "That's nuts."

Matteo nodded. "He was determined to get to the eye. He was sure that something in the eye would give him the answers to the hurricane itself. He didn't trust the satellite data anymore."

"Did he ever tell you what he was looking for?"

Matteo stood to move the boiling water back onto the stove. "He suspected that there was some kind of space program that the government was hiding. That they were launching something from the eye into the atmosphere to keep the hurricane spinning, while they launched things into space."

Miri snorted. "Are you kidding me? Like, is this area fifty-one nonsense?"

Matteo rolled his eyes. "No. Not aliens. More like space defense."

That didn't add up. "Wouldn't other countries have blown the whistle on something like that? No one can own space."

Matteo poured the hot water into his thermos and blew on it before taking a sip. "Wanna hear my theory?"

"Obviously."

"Well, after all my years inside this infernal storm, I think your dad was half right. I think they're doing something in the eye that they shouldn't, but the reason they can get away with anything is because of the hurricane itself."

Miri frowned. "What do you mean?"

"My theory is that someone made this hurricane. And if someone can do that, then they can threaten anyone with a devastating storm. So they keep Hurricane Goliath going to flex their power, and everyone else turns a blind eye to what's really going on."

Miri threw her hands up in exasperation. "No duh that someone made this storm. That's obvious by now."

Matteo shrugged and took a sip of his water. "People overlook the obvious when something is horrific. Their minds have an easier time accepting tragedy when they think the explanation is something beyond their control. Because if it was something within their control, then they might have to take responsibility."

The room fell silent again. The early morning and stress of the day was catching up with me. Not even the adrenaline from finding Matteo was helping. Miri excused herself for a nap and headed to the bathroom.

"Do you remember me?"

Matteo's question pulled me out of my daze. "Remember you?"

He smiled. "You were little the last time I saw you at an anniversary party for your parents. You were obsessed with the weather apps, and insisted on wearing suits like the meteorologists did. You called yourself 'Ashlyn Blizzard, Weather Girl,' and spent the entire party with your tech pad, trying to interview the guests on their knowledge of Hurricane Goliath."

My cheeks grew hot. "I forgot about that. It's because my favorite meteorologist, Daisy Dixon, said she used to do that when she was a kid."

Matteo laughed. "It was so cute that you had a favorite meteorologist."

I sniffed. "It's lame that no one else did."

Matteo studied my face. "Gosh, you look like your mom. Jonah would be so proud."

My throat closed up again. "You mean he *will* be so proud."

"That's right. So, I've never gone into the eye because no one has ever come out. I wasn't quite ready to lose that connection with my brother. And I thought maybe I could help if I stayed out."

I yawned. "I don't blame you."

Matteo leaned forward. "But I'll go with you. Into the eye, I mean. I'll help you find Jonah."

I always got weepy when I was exhausted, but this pushed me over the edge. I tried to hold back a sob and choked out a thin "thank you."

"And do you have a plan?" Luca growled from his spot on the bunk without turning over.

Matteo narrowed his eyes. "I think I found a back door."

The door to the shelter banged open.

CHAPTER 19

Before we had a chance to react, four people burst into our tiny shelter. Luca jumped out of the bunk and Matteo reached for me and threw me behind him. All four people pushed back their hoods and moved their goggles as the smallest person pushed the door shut. The first face I saw was Silas'. And he was not happy.

"Are you kidding me?" he barked.

My mouth dropped open, and I stepped out from behind Matteo. "How did you find us?"

Silas shot me a glare, and then his face changed. He stiffened. "Matteo?"

Matteo didn't hesitate. He ran over and grabbed Silas in a big hug, without caring that Silas was dripping wet. Silas started laughing and wrapped his arms around his brother.

The joy of watching the reunion diffused all the tension in the room. It reminded me of the videos Rosalie used to make us watch of military homecomings. She would play them at sleepovers when we were all tired and sappy and ready for a good cry. Hugh, Ginger, and Jack pushed back their hoods, and their faces seemed to be permanently fixed in grins. I stepped next to Luca, who wasn't quite so captivated by the scene.

"How *did* you find us?" Luca asked. The brothers separated and Silas turned, the scowl back on his face.

"We had to take a detour back to Ousley to get the info out of Reuben. Because that's just what we need right now. Side trips."

Jack rubbed the back of his neck. "I didn't tell them anything."

Silas glared at him. "You knew?"

He shrugged and stepped closer to me, Luca, and Miri. "Only that they left. But not where they went. I just figured if they felt like they had to sneak out in the middle of the night, then they probably had a good reason." His face reminded me of a hopeful puppy, and my stomach twisted. We should have included him. But he was the reason we got away. He helped us without knowing why.

Luca squeezed his shoulder. "Sorry, Buddy. I should have told you."

Jack grinned. "Nah, no worries. Dibs on shotgun for the next time though, okay?"

"For sure."

"No! No more of this. You kids don't seem to understand. This is not a game. You can't just go traipsing around this storm like you're on a spring break trip." Silas clenched his fists. "You owe me an explanation."

Luca stepped forward. "I think *you're* the one who owes us an explanation. How did the soldiers find us in Macon, Silas?"

Silas' face twisted with grief. "Son, you know I feel terrible about what happened."

"Don't call me Son. I mean it."

"Sorry. Luca. Yes, I have some contacts in the military. That's how I found out about the shelter. But I never expected them to show up."

Matteo groaned. "Didn't I teach you better than that? Never talk to them. USHA is dirty from the inside out. You can't trust anyone."

Indignation flashed in my chest. "Hey. My mom works for USHA. And she's not dirty."

He twisted his mouth and compassion filled his eyes. "Your mom is as good as they come. I understand she isn't intentionally doing anything wrong, but the entire organization is built on lies and exploitation. So she's kind of guilty by association."

I wanted to go home. I wanted to get Mom and Trig and Penn and Mella, and drag them all into Hurricane Goliath with me. We could camp out at these shelters on the way to the eye. And Mom would get away from USHA and Chip, and we would find Dad, and we would all live together.

Silas lowered his voice. "The best way to stop all of this is to get to the eye. We have to get the information we came for to expose everything. At the very least, the world needs awareness of what's going on. And then USHA can finally get shut down."

Luca set his jaw and glared at Silas. "Did Dad know you had contacts in the military? I've only ever heard him talk about Matteo as your contact in the storm."

Silas folded his arms. "No, he didn't, because I knew how he felt about them. He would have never taken any help that I got from them."

Luca stepped forward. "And he was right. And now he's dead." For a minute, I thought he might punch Silas.

Silas choked back a groan. "I know. I'm sorry. I'm so sorry. I just wanted our mission to be a success."

Ginger spoke for the first time since she got to the shelter. She looked furious. "So *you're* the one who told the military we were coming in? And that's why they increased security in Nashville."

Silas nodded. "I thought my guy was cool. He had been to a few Storm Chasers meetings."

I bit the inside of my cheek and glanced at Luca. He squeezed my hand and gave a slight shake of his head. Could I let Silas take the blame for this? I guess it could be true. Chip might have been acting on the intel he received from the military, rather than my slip up during that stupid confrontation.

I took comfort because while Chip may have known that the Storm Chasers were going to breach the Disaster Zone, there was no way he could know exactly where we were going. The soldiers showing up at the same time we were in Macon was not on me.

Matteo put his hand on Silas' shoulder. "What we can't do is beat ourselves up about the past. Goliath doesn't give us time for that. Let's learn and move on." He had the expression on his face that I had seen a thousand times on Trig, especially when Mella was lecturing me about something I hadn't done or hadn't done right. It was the look of a big brother.

Ginger nodded and put her pack on the table. "We're still in the window. Can we make it to the eye by Sunday?"

Matteo nodded. "We can, but if the goal is to stay away from the big shelters, then it might get tricky."

Silas narrowed his eyes. "What do you mean, 'stay away?'"

I sighed. "Minka said that Reuben told the convoy where we were stopping and when. So we can't go to the main shelters."

Silas growled. "I should have punched that guy twice."

Matteo gave a low chuckle. "Sorry about him. He really is a good, solid dude. I shouldn't have used him to take you supplies, though. I should have known that being that close to Ousley would tempt him too much."

Ginger pulled out her tech pad and opened the GPS. We crowded around the table.

"The next shelter that's not well known," Matteo said, pointing to the pad.

Jack laughed. "Zuber? What's with the names of these Florida towns?"

"Who knows? We like this shelter, though, because it's outside the main town of Ocala. But it's smaller than this one."

I looked around the room, with the eight of us jammed in there. The bunks would sleep four, and the rest would have to cram on the floor. But only if someone slept under the table, and we put the chairs in the tiny bathroom.

Luca grabbed my hand and turned to Silas. "Ash and I need to discuss this. We'll go out in the Turtle."

Silas rolled his eyes. "Come on. I'm not the enemy here."

"Maybe not, but Dad didn't trust your choices, and neither do I."

Tension filled the room again.

"Fine." Silas huffed out. "Go talk. And if you leave, we won't chase you this time. But I think you're being foolish. We can help you. We can all help each other."

Luca pulled on his goggles and pulled up his rain hood. I saw Miri stand up out of the corner of my eye, but Luca didn't look at her. He reached for the door handle, and anger flashed on Miri's face. I paused for a moment, wondering if I should include her since she left with us this morning. But I really didn't want to. I pulled down my goggles and followed Luca out into the piercing rain. The wind had kicked up even more since we got there, and I held on to Luca's arm to steady myself.

We climbed into the backseat of the Turtle, and Luca pulled the door shut.

I pushed up my goggles. "I think we should all stick together."

Luca set his mouth in a straight line. "I don't like it."

"But Matteo is going to stay with Silas now. And Matteo is the one with the information on how to get into the eye."

Luca rubbed the back of his neck and thought for a few minutes. "If we all stick together, then Silas wins."

I put my hand on Luca's leg. "Silas is right. He's not the enemy. USHA is. I mean, Chip is. And we have to do whatever it takes to stop him. If that means sticking with Silas, then I'm all for it. We're so close."

Luca grunted and laced his fingers through mine.

"And Matteo can help find my dad. Please, Luca. I can't give up a resource that might help me find him."

His eyes softened. "You're right."

I scooted closer to him. "The worst part about all this is the fact that we are all going to be sitting on top of each other for the next two days. Zero privacy."

His dimple appeared. "So, this is our last time to be alone?"

I nodded. "Do you really want to talk about Silas?"

"No, I don't." Luca leaned toward me like I hoped he would, and I lost track of the next few minutes. A particularly powerful gust from Goliath broke us apart, and I smiled.

"Come on."

We pushed our way back into the tiny shelter. Everyone had found a place to sit, and Ginger was still going over data.

"Done making out?" Silas growled. Miri folded her arms and looked at her feet.

My cheeks grew warm, and Luca scowled. "We'll stick with the group."

I cleared my throat. "But only because of Matteo."

Matteo smiled. "Stick with me, kid. We'll find Jonah."

My heartbeat picked up. This was the right call. And for the first time, I felt like the mission was to find my dad, rather than whatever the Storm Chaser agenda was. Finding out the truth about the storm was important, and could help knock Chip off of a pedestal, but only Dad could stop Mom from dating Chip.

Silas leaned forward in his chair. "Luca, I'll do whatever it takes to prove to you that I didn't get your dad killed on purpose. I mean it. Tyler and I have been partners in this since the beginning of the Storm Chasers. You may not like me much right now, but I'm going to make sure that you're okay and that you come out of this alive. For Tyler."

I glanced at Luca. He tried to keep his face neutral, but I saw the small clench of his jaw. Guilt weighed on my shoulders. At least I still had hope that Dad was alive. Luca would never have that hope again.

CHAPTER 20

Hurricane Goliath was just a storm. A rotating system of clouds and thunderstorms with sustained winds of at least seventy-four miles per hour, that formed over the tropical waters of the Gulf of Mexico fifty years ago. But today, Goliath seemed to have a soul. And a will. And Goliath's will was that we stay as far away from his eye as possible.

Silas and Matteo sat in the front of our Turtle. Luca and I sat behind them. I tried to not worry about Miri, who looked as angry as Goliath when she was relegated to the second Turtle with Hugh, Ginger, and Jack. I couldn't handle the angry emotions of two beings today. Although Hurricane Goliath wasn't exactly a being.

Ginger's voice crackled to life over the radio. "Guys, the wind...are hitting one...two."

Matteo grabbed the radio. "Silas, slow down. We have to be closer together for the radio to work. Ginger, can you repeat?"

"Wind speeds are hitting one thirty-two. Repeat, one. Three. Two."

"Copy."

I looked at Luca. "What does that mean?"

Matteo grunted. "It means Goliath is ramping back up to a Category Four."

"And it explains why I can't get the Turtle to go over sixteen miles per hour," Silas said. "I'm too busy wrestling with the steering wheel, trying to keep us on the road."

Matteo pressed the radio button. "Stay the course. We'll get there, just slower than we planned. Hugh, keep on our tail so we can stay on coms."

"Copy."

I clutched my seat as a large gust of wind rocked the Turtle. "Didn't Ginger say that we had at least five more days before Goliath hit full strength again?"

Matteo glanced back. "It's almost as if someone is controlling this storm, isn't it?"

"But if that were true, why did they let it weaken at this exact time, every ten years?"

"My theory? To let the supply convoys in. There are convoys all the time, but about every ten years they bring in a big shipment."

I tried to remember the document I had seen in Chip's office. I was mad at myself for not noticing a detail like that. "But we would have seen the supply convoy, wouldn't we? We would have been on the road at the same time."

Matteo shrugged. "They might have come in a few days before you. I wasn't looking for them. And I've stayed away from those big shelters for years, so I have no idea if they stopped at any of them."

"You knew that was a possibility, and you sent us to those shelters, anyway?" Silas asked, sounding perturbed.

"They're the best you're going to find in here. It was a risk, for sure, but this was also the time you needed to come in. With a group your size, it was the best option."

A shiver ran down my spine as I realized we might be close to Chip's goons without even realizing it. They could be within a mile of us at any point, and we wouldn't have any idea because Goliath was being such a jerk about visibility.

I sniffed. "Goliath is on Team Chip."

Luca's eyes twinkled. "What is that supposed to mean?"

"I mean, this hurricane seems to be on his side. With the increasing winds, and the way it can hide the convoy."

Silas snorted. "It's not alive, Booker."

I folded my arms. "Prove it. Something is feeding it."

Luca reached for my hand. "That's why we're going in. To kill the beast."

"Ack!" I grabbed my head. It was difficult to breathe with the pressure in my ears.

Silas swore and jerked the Turtle to the left. I gasped as I was thrown against Luca.

A massive tornado had appeared in front of us, about a half mile away. It was hard to see since the wind and rain were so intense, but the dark shape was unmistakable. The base of the tornado engulfed the road.

Matteo jumped on the radio. "There's a tornado dead ahead! Stay on our tail!"

Hugh swore over the radio. "Where are you going?"

The Turtle bumped over the squishy wet terrain. Silas pointed the Turtle toward the field. "Tell them we'll go where we won't get sucked up!"

Matteo pressed the button. "We're getting off the road!"

The Turtle hit a low spot and water splashed up over the windshield. For a second, it seemed like Silas had driven us right into a pond. He pushed forward, then the Turtle came to a stop, the wheels spinning.

"We're stuck! Go around!" Matteo shouted into the radio. But Hugh was following too close. He clipped the back of the Turtle, and we were jerked to the side. The good news was, that was the push we needed to get out of whatever rut we were stuck in. Silas put the Turtle on full power, and we lurched forward, bumping over the uneven ground.

I squeezed my eyes shut and put a death grip on the seat in front of me. The doors of the Turtle creaked, and I was afraid we were going to be crushed like a disposable cup. The Turtle rocked from side to side as a deafening roar filled the vehicle. Luca grabbed my hand, and I peeked at him. His lips moved as he said something to me, but I couldn't hear him, even though he was inches away. Hugh's Turtle was outside a few feet away from ours, but it disappeared behind a gray sheet of water blowing sideways.

Luca stopped talking and pulled me into his arms, putting a hand over my head in protection. Something cracked against the window, but the window didn't shatter. The Turtle bumped and rocked, but I couldn't tell if we were still moving forward or if we had been lifted into the tornado. I clutched the front of Luca's jumpsuit and buried my face in his neck.

Then, as if someone hit a switch, the loud roar shut off and the violent rocking settled into the regular rocking of the wind that we were used to. I automatically moved my jaw to pop my ears as Luca took his hand off of my head. I finally realized that we weren't moving, and I wondered when Silas had stopped.

Matteo looked over his shoulder. "Is everyone all right?"

I looked up into Luca's face, and relief filled his eyes. He pressed a soft kiss to my forehead. "Yeah, we're fine."

I twisted out of his arms and peered out the window. Hugh's Turtle was still there. "I can't believe that happened."

Silas sat back and rubbed his neck. "I can. I'm just mad that it took me by surprise."

Matteo pushed the button on the radio. "Everyone okay over there?"

"Yes. Jack got a nasty bump on his head, but he'll live."

Luca grinned. "It's not the first time. The kid has a hard noggin."

Silas grabbed the radio. "Ginger, can you pinpoint our location? I'm all turned around."

The radio was silent for a full minute, which felt much longer. It was hard to believe that we could be lost; there was nothing around except brown, wet hills. But the wind and rain made it difficult to see very far, and we could point ourselves in the wrong direction and drive for hours.

Ginger's voice finally came over the radio. "The road should be about a mile directly behind us."

Silas grunted. "Should be. That fills me with confidence."

Matteo rolled his eyes. "You guys depend too much on technology. You gotta learn how to navigate Goliath without someone holding your hand. You took a hard right off the road, right? And when we were on the road, the wind was pushing on us from the left. So we have to head directly back into the wind to find the road, then make sure the wind is hitting our left side again. That's how we know we're headed south."

"Impressive," I said. "Any tips on how to see those tornados before they're on top of us like that?"

"No. I've never seen a tornado in here."

My heart sank. "So, it wasn't coincidence that we just happened to find one on the road?"

He shook his head. "There are no coincidences inside Goliath. Which means the smart thing to do is to get off of I-75. It's safe to say at this point, USHA knows where we're headed, and I-75 is the only road to the eye."

My throat squeezed shut. I hated that Chip had all the power. I took a deep breath and rested my head back on the seat as Silas turned the Turtle around and drove straight into the wind. Maybe when we got to the road, we should point ourselves north. It wasn't worth risking everyone's lives.

"Cheer up, Weather Girl," Matteo said. "We're almost to Zuber. We dodged one tornado; we can do it again."

"Weather Girl?" Silas snorted.

I rolled my eyes. "Don't worry about it. Hey!" An idea popped up, one that was unearthed by the memory of my days of being obsessed with meteorology. "We can guess when a tornado is coming."

Matteo looked at me and smiled, as if he had expected me to come up with something. "How?"

"The pressure. It will drop really fast. Did you feel that in your ears just before we saw it?"

Silas leaned forward, as if that would help the Turtle move into the wind faster. "Yeah, but it was seconds between that and when we saw it. How will that help us?"

"Ginger can watch it on the tech pad. I bet there's a drop sooner than we feel it. Or I can. I know how to read barometric pressures."

Silas grunted. "If you think you can, then do it. I want Ginger on GPS."

Luca handed me a pad. "Do your thing, Booker. I'll watch."

My innards warmed at the twinkle in Luca's eye, and I pulled up Ginger's meteorological program. For the first time on our mission, I wasn't dead weight, hitching a ride until I found Dad. I had a purpose. And I could help get us to the eye. And, most importantly, I could fight back against whatever Chip threw at us.

"What do we do if we see a tornado coming? Are we going to get thrown off the road every time?" Luca asked.

Matteo twisted his mouth. "Let's try getting a few hundred yards off the road. I have a theory these things are programmed to follow the road, so we don't need to go so far."

The thought of being so close to a tornado should have terrified me, but I was excited. This would be data to use against USHA. "Luca, when the next one comes, you should video it. We should keep a record."

Luca nodded and pulled out his com. It took thirty solid minutes to get back to the road, when it had taken mere seconds to get off the road. Silas alternated between pushing the Turtle to full power and backing off so that he didn't overload the engine.

Matteo said that we were about ten miles from Zuber. That should have taken us thirty minutes. But two miles down the road, the barometric pressure dropped quickly, so we drove off the road the length of a football field. As soon as we stopped, a funnel dropped out of the sky onto the road and moved north. The whole thing took less than five minutes, but cost us another fifteen to get back to the road.

This happened two more times before we reached Zuber. I was almost sad that we had made it. I loved dodging the tornados. The look on Chip's face would be priceless if he knew that his dumb tornados weren't keeping us from our mission.

Silas slowed to a stop before we reached the shelter. A humvee sat chained to the anchor post outside. The humvee looked like it had gone a few rounds with Goliath already and didn't quite win any of them.

"Any idea who that might be?" Silas asked.

Matteo leaned forward, and his mouth dropped open. "That's Jonah's."

All the breath left my body as I reached for the Turtle door. Dad was here? I didn't even remember to pull up the hood of my rain jumpsuit as I fumbled with the handle. Luca grabbed my hand.

"Hold on, Booker. Wait."

"But he's here!"

He reached over and guided my chin so I was looking at him. "He might be here. But we have to be safe."

"Let me get closer to the shelter," Silas said. "I don't want to use the harnesses, and there's no need to get blown away trying to run over there. And then we'll make a plan. Let's think this through."

I couldn't believe what I was hearing. "What do you mean, make a plan? You mean more than going inside and finding my dad?"

Matteo looked over his shoulder. "Ashlyn, I haven't seen him in three years. That looks like his humvee, but it doesn't mean that he's the one who drove it here. We don't know who is inside that shelter. And it's not that big, so we need to be smart."

Silas pulled up next to the shelter and radioed to Hugh that we needed to assess the situation before heading in.

Luca squeezed my hand. "Let me go in. Please? I'll check and come right back out for you."

Silas nodded. "I'll go with Luca. We have the guns. Matteo, you and Ashlyn stay in the Turtle. That way, if anything happens, you guys can get out of here."

I wanted to scream. "This is ridiculous."

Luca leaned in. "No, it's not. If there's someone in there who is going to hurt us, then you need to be able to get away to go find your dad. But if it's a friendly, then I'll be right out. It's a win-win for you."

Matteo nodded. "This is best. It's just a few minutes. The end will be the same; we're going to find your dad. If he's here, then we're done. If he's not, then we'll go. Okay?"

My heart rate slowed at their logic. For a moment, though, fear took over. "Luca, be careful."

Silas gave a wry smile. "I'll go in first, okay? That way, I'll be the first hit, if that's what they're going to do."

"Let go of my hand, Booker," Luca said. "The sooner we go, the sooner we'll know."

I made myself let him go, and Luca and Silas pulled down their goggles and pulled up their hoods. They jumped out of the Turtle and pressed through the wind to the door. Silas pushed the door open, and he and Luca disappeared inside, the door slamming shut.

The seconds dragged by as I stared at that door. How long was I going to have to wait? One thing was certain;

I would not leave without knowing what happened inside that shelter.

"This is stupid. I'm going in." I pulled down my goggles.

"Wait." Matteo leapt over the seat and grabbed my arm. "One more minute. Ashlyn, think of your dad."

I tried to jerk my arm away. "Don't lecture me on my dad! I've been waiting for him for ten years. And I'm tired of people standing in my way, telling me I can't get to him."

"But we will! I promise! Look!"

The door to the shelter opened, and Luca ran out into the rain to our Turtle. He threw open the Turtle door.

CHAPTER 21

"Not your dad." Luca had to shout to be heard over Goliath's roar. My throat caught at his words, but I was so grateful that he didn't drag it out.

"A friendly?" Matteo asked.

"Yes!" Luca shouted back. He waved at us to follow, then hurried to chain up the Turtle. Matteo radioed to Hugh that it was safe to enter, and we both pulled down our goggles and headed into Goliath.

I burst inside, and Silas was standing next to the door. A woman sat at the tiny table. This shelter was even smaller than the one in Traxler. There was one double bed and a table that had two chairs.

The woman scowled. "How many of you did you say there are?"

Silas grinned. "Eight."

She huffed. "Great. And are you sure you have to stay here?" She twisted her long hair into a knot on top of her head, and I realized she wasn't a woman. She was a girl. Probably younger than me.

"Who are you?" I asked.

She rolled her eyes. "Who are *you*?"

Silas jumped in. "Let's wait for the team before we do introductions, okay? It'll be less annoying that way."

She slumped in her chair. "Newsflash. You can't make this less annoying."

I almost laughed out loud. She reminded me so much of Gretchen. A wave of sadness washed over me as I thought about my friends for the first time in days. I should have been sharing a nice, plush cabin with Gretchen, Rosalie, and Dasha. There were beds and couches and blankets for all of us. The camp resort our class was staying at was in the woods right outside of downtown Seattle, and was supposed to give us the best of both worlds. Rosalie had loaded a ton of old rom coms for us to cast on the wall screen every night. Dasha had made a rule that no one could be in our cabin if they weren't wearing pajama pants.

I squeezed myself into the corner of the shelter as the rest of the team poured in. This was going to be rough.

Jack was the last one in, and pulled the door shut behind him. He turned around and caught sight of the girl at the table. He pushed up his goggles. "Well, hello."

The girl lit up. "Hey."

I looked back and forth between the two. The girl seemed to relax, and Jack had a grin on his face that made him appear more mature than I had ever seen him.

Silas read the situation and took a step back. "Jack, why don't you introduce our team?"

Jack stood up taller. "I'm Jack. This is Silas, Hugh, Ginger, Miri, Ashlyn, Matteo, and Luca."

The girl smiled at Jack. Only at Jack. "I'm Cyra."

"Hey, Cyra." Jack sat down at the table next to her. She leaned forward, flirt written all over her face.

Silas cleared his throat and Jack looked startled, as if he had forgotten we were there.

"Oh! Uh, so, uh, why are you here?" The normal goofy expression that Jack usually had returned to his face. His cheeks turned red.

Cyra laughed. "Well, I'm not on vacation or anything. I'm just stopping for the night."

The smooth, flirt look returned to Jack's face. "It's not even close to night."

Cyra rolled her eyes. "Duh, dummy. But that old dinosaur has to charge for, like, ten hours. I don't think it had a full charge when I left, and I didn't want to risk it dying somewhere where I didn't have shelter."

"Twelve."

Cyra cast a suspicious eye at Matteo. "What?"

Matteo folded his arms. "It takes twelve hours to charge that humvee."

She glanced around the room, as if calculating how much she wanted to say. "And how do you know that?"

"Because that's not your humvee."

"Is it yours?"

Matteo kept a steady gaze. "I know who it belongs to. Do you?"

This back and forth, with everyone asking questions and no one answering them, was getting to me. I couldn't help it. I exploded. "Does it belong to Jonah Booker or not?"

Cyra's mouth dropped open before she could school her features. "Why? Do you know him? Because I don't know you."

I narrowed my eyes. "Do *you* know him?"

Silas threw his hands in the air. "We are getting nowhere. Let's make this more productive. Hi Cyra, we're the Storm

Chasers. We are on a mission to reach the eye. This is Ashlyn Booker, Jonah Booker's daughter."

Matteo jumped in. "I know that's Jonah's humvee, because I helped him prep it ten years ago, before he entered the storm."

Cyra stared at me. "You're Jonah's daughter?"

The way she said it filled me with hope. "Yes! Do you know him?"

The scowl appeared on her face. "Yeah, I do. Why do you think I'm here? To get away from *him*."

Questions erupted from all over the room.

"Is he alive?"

"Did you come from the eye?"

"When did you leave?"

"How did you get out?"

"When did you get to the eye?"

"How old are you?"

I jumped up on the bed. "Is he alive?"

Everyone finally stopped talking. Cyra heaved out a huge sigh. "Yes, he's alive. At least he was two days ago when I stole his car. And you're getting my bed wet. I *am* sleeping in the bed. I was here first."

I sat down. "He is?"

Cyra pursed her lips and studied me. "Yes. I promise. But he's the reason I left, so I can't, like, pretend like I like him or anything."

Luca sat next to me and grabbed my hand. "Ashlyn hasn't seen him in ten years. We came into the storm looking for him."

Cyra sniffed. "Wow, that's rough."

"Can you tell us how you got out of the eye? Because I have never heard of anyone who has ever gotten out of the eye." Matteo leaned against the door as if he had all the time in the world to chat.

Confusion covered Cyra's face. "What do you mean, no one has gotten out? It's not a prison. No one leaves because no one *wants* to leave. It's some kind of utopia in there or something. At least, that's what my parents alway say."

We all looked at each other, trying to process this.

"So, you just left?" Matteo asked. "No one tried to stop you?"

Cyra folded her arms. "Well, I mean I drove out of the tunnel. But I ran away from my parents. I didn't want to live my whole life in there, you know? I get it, no crime, no disease, no *fun*. I doubt the rest of the world is such a dumpster fire, and I was tired of waiting for permission. So I took Jonah's car and left."

"How old are you?" Ginger asked.

"Why does that matter?"

"Just because we're curious. Were you born in the eye?"

Cyra looked at Ginger like she had asked if it was raining outside. "Uh, yeah. Of course. And I'm old enough to leave home, okay? I mean, if I'm old enough to be forced to pick a career path, then I'm old enough to decide what to do with my life."

Jack leaned back in his chair and draped his arm over the seatback, once again taking on the posture of a guy who felt confident with the ladies.

"I'm seventeen. I'm the youngest on the team, but we don't care about age. How old are you?"

Cyra's cheeks flushed. "I'm sixteen."

Miri's mouth dropped open. "They make you choose a career path at sixteen? Jeez, what's the rush?"

Cyra's eyes opened wide. "Because we have to contribute to society. I mean, there are only five thousand people there. They want everyone to work as soon as possible. And once you pick a path, you can't ever leave it. Ever. They don't have time to retrain anyone. Why are you asking this? Is that not how they do it outside?"

Miri let out a derisive laugh. "Heck no. In fact, most kids have no idea what they're going to do with their life until they're, like, twenty-five. So they live at home and work dumb jobs until they figure it out."

I snorted. "Some people know what they want," I said under my breath. The talk of the future ripped open a wound I had almost forgotten about. Mason had known what he wanted to do with his life. So much so that he told me he didn't want to have to think about me while he worked on it.

Luca squeezed my hand. "Forget about him. Remember? Not worth it."

I smiled at him. I was so glad he was here.

"You two together?" Cyra asked. I realized then that the whole group had overheard me and was watching our exchange. This tiny shelter was really going to be the worst.

"Uh." My ears warmed at the sight of the amused smirks on the faces of most of the team, and the scowl on the face of Miri.

Luca faced them all head on, with his dimple in place. "Yeah. We are."

Cyra shook her head. "That's another reason I'm trying to get out of here. Jonah kept telling me I wasn't good enough for anyone in the City. But guess what? Those dumb boys weren't good enough for me. I knew there had to be better guys out there somewhere."

Jack's face lit up. "So, you don't have a boyfriend?"

Silas cleared his throat. "We can all have this sleepover chat later. Right now, we need information so we can make a plan."

Cyra huffed and leaned back. "What plan?"

"We're still going into the eye. And it sounds like you got out okay, so we need to know if we can go in the way you came out."

Cyra shrugged. "I just drove out of the tunnel and down the road. I saw this shelter, and I needed to charge the dumb car. So I pulled over."

"But where was the tunnel?" Matteo asked.

"At the end of the road?"

Ginger pulled out her tech pad and pulled up the GPS. "Can you point to it on the map?"

Cyra stared at the screen. "Um, I've never seen a map like this. We have the map of our city. And I've seen a map of the world. But they never told us about roads and things outside the eye. I just knew I had to go north."

The mixture of advancement and ignorance that Cyra seemed to possess was fascinating. She talked about a place where there was no crime or disease, yet didn't know anything about the world outside the eye. I felt a little bad for her, but I also wanted her to give me information about Dad. So I stepped in. "Look, we're headed to Minneola, right? But we have to get off of the Florida Turnpike to do it. The Florida Turnpike leads into Orlando."

Cyra looked impressed. "Yeah, that's right. The Florida Turnpike."

"So, we skip the Minneola shelter, and head right on in tomorrow?" Silas asked.

My heart picked up the pace. I was going to see Dad tomorrow.

Matteo narrowed his eyes. "Is it true? We can drive right in?"

Cyra gave Matteo a confused look. "Why wouldn't you? The storm is what keeps people out. It's what keeps people in, too."

For the first time, Cyra sounded young. I leaned forward. "Will you take us in?"

Cyra shook her head. "No. Way. I'm not going back. I'm sick of Jonah making all these rules for us to follow. I know he's your dad and all, but I'm sorry. He's a real dictator. It took me forever to find the right time to leave, and I only have another day or so before they realize I went into the storm. That's probably how long it will take them to search the City. I have to keep going."

Jack put his hand on Cyra's arm. "It's not safe, though. They're using the storm to spawn tornados to sweep the highway."

Cyra swore. "It's probably Pax. He didn't want me to go. I bet he's trying to scare me into going back. How did you get by them?"

"So, the tornados *are* being manufactured?" Matteo asked, his eyes lighting up.

"Of course they are. Pax chose to go the Weather Production route, and he thinks he's so cool. I bet he broke into the control room. He wanted me to stay, but I just couldn't. And he refused to come with me."

I thought quickly. "We got by them using weather data. But we can't give you this tech. How about you lead us back, and then we'll take you back with us when we leave?"

Cyra looked surprised. "You're going to leave? You mean, you're not trying to break in and take over?"

"Of course we're going to leave. We're on a mission, and we just want to gather the data we're looking for, and find my dad, and then we're headed home."

Her eyes grew. "They always told us that the storm was meant to keep people out, so they wouldn't drain our resources. That if everyone knew about our city, they would all want to come, and we couldn't support them. I never thought anyone wouldn't want to stay."

Jack grinned. "This sounds like a magical city. I really want to see it now. Come on, please take us? And then you can come back with me. My grandma will let you stay with her in Colorado. She makes the best homemade cookies. She uses real, separate ingredients, not the convenience kits."

Cyra smiled for the first time since we met. "Colorado? That state still exists? Heck yes! I'm in, but only if you promise to take me back."

Silas nodded. "Sure."

"Okay, well, I still have to charge my car."

I squeezed Luca's hand. This was happening. With Cyra leading us, it would be a straight shot into the eye. We could finally beat Goliath.

CHAPTER 22

CYRA SLUMPED DOWN IN her seat. Her arms were folded, and she had her hood pulled down over her face as far as it could go. Which meant it barely reached her eyes. Did I act that immature when I was sixteen? Trig would have been more than happy to tell me.

I stuffed down the wave of homesickness that threatened to overtake me when I thought of Trig and shifted so Cyra could have a little more space. We had convinced her to leave Dad's humvee at the shelter in Zuber. We used some extra chains from the Turtles to secure it so it would still be there when we came back. We needed her help to get into the eye, and so I made it my job to keep her happy. Which was proving to be harder than moving through Goliath.

I dug in my bag. "Anyone need a snack? I have a few of the good energy bars left." I had come a long way in my love for the dry cardboard food bars. Hugh had been right; they took some getting used to. But now that they were all I had to eat, I had developed a fondness for them.

Matteo turned in his seat. "Ooo, the cherry ones? Yes, please."

"Cyra?"

She wrinkled her nose. "Is that what you guys eat outside the storm? For real?"

I gave a little laugh. "We've only been eating them on this mission. They're not the greatest, but they get the job done. And some taste better than others."

Luca leaned forward to look at Cyra past me. "On the outside, we eat real food. Well, Dad and I usually ate meal pods, but only because we're lazy."

I watched his face as he mentioned his dad. He seemed okay, so I turned back to Cyra. "I have cherry, oatmeal cookie, and peanut butter left. Do you want one? The cherry ones are the best, and the peanut butter is my least favorite, but that's just my preference."

Cyra took a cherry bar, peeled back the wrapping, and took a nibble. Her eyes brightened, and she took a big bite. This girl had no guile; everything she felt showed up on her face.

I decided to risk asking a few questions. "So, will you tell me how you met my dad?"

She scowled, as if the cherry bar had turned sour in her mouth. "He's, like, my parents' BFF. I've known him since I was a little kid."

"Do they work together?"

Cyra shrugged. "I guess so. He comes over, like, every weekend to hang out with my dad. And they always make me go to my room or send me to watch a video while they talk about stuff."

Luca grinned. "What do they talk about?"

She took another bite of the bar, then spoke around the food in her mouth. "It's usually pretty boring. They spend a lot of time talking about the Weather Production Center. They sound like they're trying to, like, score points with someone because it always sounds like they are making plans to increase output. I don't know. I've never cared about that stuff. Mostly I try to listen in, because Pax is the mayor's son, and I want to hear what they're saying about the mayor."

"Who is the mayor?" Matteo asked. "Is he the person in charge of everything?"

Cyra wrinkled her forehead. "Duh. I mean, who else would be in charge? Also, the mayor is a she, not a he. Adele Renwick. She's the worst."

"How so?"

"She has all of these rules for Pax. And I can tell she doesn't like me. She's always trying to tell me that Pax is too busy to hang out, and that if I really liked him, then I'd let him do his thing, and not get in his way." Cyra sniffed. "Whatever. Pax isn't that great. He's, like, all in on the City and stuff. He wasn't worth the fight."

A chill ran down my spine at the all-too-familiar scenario. Mrs. Woods was the same way. And she won by convincing Mason to break up with me. Were moms of sons always this overbearing? Mom didn't act like that with Trig and Penn.

A huge gust of wind rocked the Turtle, and Cyra's eyes grew wide. I checked the tech pad. "Don't worry. Barometric pressure is holding steady. No tornadoes right now."

Cyra relaxed and finished her energy bar. "That was good. Thanks."

Luca reached over and grabbed my hand. "So, what's your beef with Jonah?"

My heart rate quickened. I squeezed Luca's hand and shot him a smile. My mind buzzed with questions about the city, but all I wanted to know was what happened to Dad. He gave me a quick wink.

Cyra watched us, a cynical smirk stretched across her face. "You are so obvious, trying to get answers for your girlfriend."

I turned to her. "Here's my story: my dad went missing in Hurricane Goliath ten years ago. Right after I turned eight. All they would tell me was that he had a theory about the storm, and he wanted to go in the storm to study it. Right around that time, USHA had cut most of the funding on storm research, but Dad got his mission approved. Then they lost contact thirty miles in. And, like, two days later, they declared him Missing in Action, and they called off the search."

Sadness filled Cyra's eyes. That surprised me. I wasn't sure she was capable of empathy. "Oh. Well, that's sad."

I wanted to capitalize on her emotions. "Yeah, it was. And the worst part was, the guy who called off the search? The head of USHA? His name is Chip Sinclair. And last month, at my birthday dinner, he and my mom told us they were dating. And he wants to marry her and run for president."

Her mouth dropped open. "You still have presidents out there?"

I tried to mask my disappointment. That's what she took away from all that? But she wasn't blowing me off, so I tried to take that as a win. "Yeah. We still vote and all that. So anyway, I've always believed that Dad was still alive. Everyone else has just accepted that he's dead, and isn't coming back. But he has to. He has to stop Mom from marrying Chip. And we have to stop Chip from using Goliath to further his career."

Cyra folded her arms and slumped back in her seat as she studied my face. "Okay, I guess I get all that. Blech. It's just hard to think of Jonah as being, like, a normal dad or something."

My heart sank. "Didn't he ever talk about his family?"

She stared out the window. "I don't know. Look, I didn't really pay that much attention. All I know is that he was like, buddy buddy with my parents, and yet he was always saying stuff to me about how I shouldn't even be there, and how I had no future and would never make it and stuff."

I was so confused. That didn't make any sense. My dad was *not* a mean person. "Are you sure?"

She snorted. "Yeah, I'm sure. He used to say stuff like that to all the kids. He volunteered at our youth centers, and all the adults there just loved him, but he was always so mean to us kids behind their backs. And no one would ever believe us, either."

My stomach twisted. I know I was young when Dad left, but I just didn't remember him being mean. Mella, Trig, and Penn never said he was mean either. Did going into Goliath change him?

Luca put his hand on my leg. "Don't worry. We'll find him, and we'll figure this out."

Matteo leaned back over the seat. "Tell us more what it's like inside your city."

"It's just a city," Cyra said. "I mean, I guess it's clean. They told us that before Goliath, all the cities in the mainland were absolute dumps, filled with garbage and homeless people and crime. They always made a big deal out of how clean our city is. And they said by now that the mainland states had probably devolved into segregated areas that fought, like way back when the Native American tribes lived without the white people. In school, we learned that the United States government most likely collapsed within the last ten years."

My jaw dropped. "That is crazy."

Cyra shrugged. "It's a cautionary tale of the inevitable end of democracy. If people have the right to choose, then eventually they'll gravitate toward only those who agree with them. That leads to the breakdown of society. So it's best if you have more of a dynasty in place, where the same family leads and trains up their family members to continue the leadership."

Luca narrowed his eyes. "So that's how your city is? Your mayor got the job because she was born into it?"

"Yeah. The Renwick family founded our city by gathering all the survivors when they were cut off from the rest of the states by Goliath. They organized food and shelter for everyone, and reallocated jobs if there were vacant ones because of the people who evacuated."

I shook my head. "Sounds like a weird monarchy. Didn't the United States fight a war to be free of something like that?"

Cyra laughed. "No, they fought because they were being taxed without representation. Our city is great, because we're all within twenty miles, so it's easy to get to City Hall to let the Renwicks know what we need. They're very fair. Adele is our second mayor. Her dad, Geno, instated her as mayor when she turned thirty-five last year."

Silas spoke up for the first time on our trip. "Sounds like paradise. Why did you leave again?"

Cyra sighed. "Because I didn't want to pick a job. I have no idea what I want to do. And I wanted to see the world. I thought if I could get out, maybe I'd learn something. And besides, Jonah kept telling me I was too dumb for any job the City had, and he was always at my house hanging with my parents."

A loud beep sounded from my tech pad. "Oh, crap! The pressure is dropping fast!" As soon as the words left my mouth, Silas jerked the wheel to the right.

Matteo jumped on the radio. "Tornado, dead ahead! Move!"

Cyra screamed and grabbed the handle over her head. We had barely bumped off the road when the narrow funnel roared behind us. The back end of the Turtle lifted, then slammed back down.

Within seconds, it was gone. Silas turned around. "Is everyone okay?"

Luca glanced at Cyra and me. "Yeah, I think so."

Matteo pressed the button on the radio. "Everyone okay back there?"

Silence.

Matteo and Silas exchanged glances. "Hugh? Respond. Are you all okay?"

After ten more seconds of radio silence, Silas put the Turtle in gear and made a wide circle to face the road.

The second Turtle wasn't there.

CHAPTER 23

LUCA FUMBLED FOR THE door handle. I grabbed his arm.

"Stop! What are you doing?"

"I'm going to find the Turtle!" he snapped.

Matteo jumped out of his seat to block Luca, which was hard to do in the cramped quarters. "You can't go out there. You'll get blown away."

I tapped on the tech pad. "The wind speed is one hundred and forty-nine right now. You can't go out in an open field. Not even with a harness."

Luca hyperventilated. "But we have to find them. I have to find Miri!"

My heart sank at the panic on his face. Miri was the one he was worried about? Was she more than a friend, and he finally realized that?

A muffled sob on the other side of me tore my attention away from Luca. I had almost forgotten about Cyra. She still had a death grip on her handle, and her face was white. Tears streamed down her cheeks.

I put my hand on Luca's leg to make sure he would stay in place and turned to Cyra. "Are you okay?"

She closed her eyes and took a shuddering breath. "Was that a tornado?"

"Yes. Haven't you ever seen one?"

She shook her head. "No. I mean, not a real one. I've seen the computer models, of course, in our weather production classes in school. But I didn't know that's what they did."

"What did you think they did?"

"I don't know. They were just different forms of wind. There's wind all around us all the time. They told us that the tornados kept debris away from our borders."

I glanced over at her and realized she was fine, physically. She could wait. I turned back to Luca. My breath caught in my throat. Tears streamed down his cheeks.

"Luca?" I tried to grab his hand, but he didn't respond. It was like holding a dead fish.

"Is she gone?"

"Miri?"

He looked at me, his eyes wide with sorrow. "What if she's gone? She's, like, the only family I have left."

My heart broke. I had no words. Had it really only been four days since Tyler was killed? Luca hadn't seemed to mourn the loss of his dad. Maybe the losing Miri was the thing that would push him over the edge.

I gave his hand a little squeeze. "You still have your mom."

Luca shook his head. "I'm never going to see her again. We're not going to make it back."

Silas turned. "We *are* going to make it back. I promise."

Luca gave a mirthless laugh. "You can't make that promise."

"I just did. And I don't break promises. Now, let's keep going. Booker, you've got to keep a better eye on that pressure."

I swallowed hard. "I will, but I'm not sure it'll help. I mean, I was watching it the whole time. I took my eyes off the pad for about two seconds, and the pressure tanked. That tornado formed and dropped faster than it was supposed to. I should have seen the pressure dropping for at least a full minute before the funnel appeared."

Cyra stared at the window. "Oh. They did it. R and D had been working on ways to speed up the tornado process. They said it took a lot of energy to slowly form a tornado, and that a quick burst might save energy in the long run."

A rock formed in my stomach. "How can we move forward? Are we trapped?"

Silas and Matteo looked at each other for a long moment. Finally Silas spoke. "We have to keep going. How far are we from the tunnel?"

Matteo rubbed the back of his neck. "About fifteen miles out."

Silas nodded and turned on full power to the Turtle. He eased it back on the road. "We'll make it."

I looked at Luca, who had his head buried in his hands. I couldn't help him right now. "I've got my eyes on the pad. I'll give you constant updates. If the pressure drops at all, be ready, Silas. No matter what."

Silas nodded. "I'll be ready."

Cyra took her hand off of the handle. "We should have at least thirty minutes. They've never been able to create another tornado within thirty minutes of the last one."

Matteo shot a relieved glance over his shoulder. "Well, that's good news."

Silas gripped the steering wheel. "I'm going to push it for thirty minutes. That should get us over halfway there, anyway."

No one spoke as Silas pushed the Turtle forward. At twenty-eight minutes, the barometric pressure blipped down and back up within a second. But we were ready for it. At twenty-nine minutes, Silas eased the Turtle about fifty yards off the road. He positioned the Turtle so we were facing the road, which gave us a perfect view of the funnel that dropped out of the sky exactly thirty minutes after the last one. It followed the road for about a half mile before giving up and jumping back into the sky.

"Thanks, Cyra," I said.

She looked at me with sad eyes. "For what?"

"For the intel. You saved us."

She swallowed hard. "But I didn't save Jack."

Silas pushed the Turtle back onto the road. "I'm not ready to write off the other Turtle just yet. I think they just got thrown somewhere. These Turtles are practically indestructible."

Luca scoffed. "But the people inside aren't."

Matteo pressed the button on the radio. "Hugh? Do you copy?"

Silence.

He looked back at us, determination on his face. "Let's get to the eye. As soon as we get you to your dad, Ashlyn, I'll bring a Turtle back out to look for them."

For the first time since the first tornado, Luca looked hopeful. "I'll come with you."

I swallowed my disappointment. I wanted Luca to stay with me. But I tried to not get ahead of myself.

"Whoa. What are those?" Silas slowed the Turtle. Massive concrete pillars appeared on each side of the road. They were each about as wide as the Turtle and as high as a four story building. They sat about five hundred feet apart.

Cyra brightened. "Oh good. We're almost there. There won't be any tornados from here on."

"Are you sure?" I checked the tech pad. "Whoa. Hang on. The wind speed is only at a hundred and two right here."

"Yeah. These pillars have the lasers in them. They maintain the eyewall."

I stared out the windshield. "So, we're in the eyewall?"

She shook her head. "No, we're past that. The lasers are right inside. They're, like, the fence." I was a little disappointed. I had been so focused on watching for tornadoes that I had missed the eyewall.

Silas slammed on the brakes, and I was thrown forward.

"Cyra. I thought you said you just drove out of the tunnel, and no one was there to stop you." He sounded angry.

"I did." She leaned around to get a look out the front window.

A large black humvee blocked the road.

"Who is that?"

Cyra frowned, then relaxed. "Oh, that's a maintenance humvee. They go out to the laser pillars to work on them."

Silas tapped on his wheel. "Will they let us through?"

She shrugged.

"Okay, let's think of a cover story," Matteo said.

"Or I could just try to drive around them," Silas replied.

I glanced at the tech pad again. "Whoa. The wind just dropped to fifty miles per hour."

Cyra looked at the pad. "Oh yeah. They can slow the wind so people can get out and move around. To let the workers into the pillars."

A man jumped out of the humvees.

"Do the workers always carry rifles?" Silas asked.

Cyra frowned. "What's a rifle?"

"A gun. A weapon?"

"No way. No one has guns in the City. Because we don't have crime." Her mouth dropped open. "Wait, is that stick called a rifle?"

Silas gripped the wheel. "Well? What's our story?"

"We're part of the supply convoy?" Matteo suggested.

Cyra wrinkled her nose. "What's a supply convoy?"

Matteo turned around. "The big vehicles that bring you supplies?"

She shook her head. "We don't get supplies. We have everything we need."

I turned to her. "That's not true. USHA sends in supplies every month. And we think that every ten years, they send in extra supplies, and that's why Goliath downgrades to a Category Three. To make for easier passage."

Cyra looked confused. "I don't think that happens. We would know."

Silas sighed. "Well, here he comes. It's the only story we got. So we're part of the supply convoy, okay? Let me do the talking. This won't work if everyone is coming up with different stories. Everyone, put on your goggles." We all did what he asked, and Cyra slid down behind Silas's seat to hide.

The man approached the Turtle. Silas lowered the window. "Hey, guys. What's up?"

"Who are you?"

"We're with the supply convoy. Did they already come through? We got separated a while back, near Ousley."

The man studied Silas. "They came through four days ago. You couldn't have gotten that separated."

Cyra's mouth dropped, and I put my hand out to remind her to be quiet.

Silas snorted. "Well, those tornado guard dogs did nothing to help. We've got the medical supplies, so are you going to let us through?"

The man leaned forward and looked in Silas's window, taking in the four of us in the Turtle. "I've got to call this in. Wait here." He walked back to his humvee and Silas raised his window.

"Now what?" Matteo asked.

Silas checked the dashboard of the Turtle. "I could just gun it. He's not back in his vehicle yet. We might be able to outrun him."

Matteo shook his head. "He'd just radio ahead."

"Well, what's your idea?" For the first time, the two sounded like brothers. They reminded me so much of Trig and Penn. Silas was Penn with his crazy ideas, and Matteo was Trig with his logic and natural disdain for any idea his younger brother had.

I turned to Cyra. "Did you know him?"

She shook her head. "I've never seen him before. I mean, there *are* five thousand people in our city, so I don't know everyone, but I thought I knew everyone on this side of town. And why did he have a weapon?"

Dread curled around my spine. "I bet he's one of Chip's goons."

Our radio crackled to life. "...over?"

I gasped. "Is that the other Turtle?" Luca popped forward, as if he were going to grab the radio.

Matteo snatched up the radio. "Repeat?"

"I have an unknown vehicle at the northwestern tunnel. How should I proceed, over?"

Luca slumped back. "Oh."

Silas grinned. "Tell him to let us through."

The radio crackled again. "I repeat, I have an unknown vehicle at the northwestern tunnel. How should I proceed, over?"

Matteo pressed the button. "Who is this?"

Silas grinned. "Are you messing with him?"

Matteo shrugged and smiled.

"This is Wendall, over."

"Let them through, Wendall. You're wasting our time. We expected those vehicles from the convoy four days ago."

"It's just one vehicle, sir. Over."

"Enough with the over. Send it through. And if the other one shows up, send that through too. Who else do you think would knock on our door?"

"Sorry, sir. Will do. Over."

"Stop wasting our time."

"Sorry sir. Over."

Matteo put down the radio with a grin. "There. And now when the other Turtle shows up, they'll be able to get through too."

Luca gave a ghost of a smile. "If they show up."

"When." Silas turned around. "I'll put my money on Hugh every time."

I leaned forward and handed Matteo another cherry energy bar. "That was amazing. Here, you can have my last cherry bar."

Matteo took it and smiled. "I've fooled a few of those convoys during my time in Goliath. These guards are always the same. Just following orders. They never seem to question who is giving the orders."

Wendall came back to our Turtle, and Silas lowered the window. "Well?"

Wendall cleared his throat. "You're clear. Sorry about that. I had to check."

"No worries, man," Silas said. "You're doing a great job. I appreciate it."

Wendall puffed up his chest and nodded. "Enjoy your time in the City."

Silas gave a thumbs up and raised the window. He powered up the Turtle and moved forward. Cyra popped up and slid back into her seat as soon as we were out of Wendall's sight. A half mile down the road was a large cement tunnel.

My breathing quickened. "Is this it? Are we there?"

Cyra nodded and sighed. "Yeah. I had hoped to never see this again."

I gave her a smile. "I'm really glad you came, though. You helped us make it."

She rolled her eyes, as if uncomfortable with praise. "Whatever. Just don't forget your promise. You're taking me with you when you guys leave again."

Silas nodded. "I remember."

He pushed the Turtle forward, and we eased into the darkness of the tunnel. To my surprise, I couldn't see the end. Lights turned on as we pushed through and turned off behind us. After about three minutes of driving this way, I saw the light at the end of the tunnel.

Luca grabbed my hand, and butterflies filled my stomach. I wasn't sure if the butterflies were because Luca had reached out to me for the first time since we lost the other Turtle, or if they were because I was going to see my dad.

The Turtle exited the tunnel into sunshine and blue sky. We hadn't seen the sky since Nashville.

Silas stopped the Turtle. "Okay. Now what?"

CHAPTER 24

THE SUNSHINE HURT MY eyes. I guess all it took was six days in the storm's darkness to have our bodies adjust to living in less light. I pulled my goggles back down, and they shifted into a darkened mode that made them like sunglasses.

Cyra leaned over the seat. "Well? Where do you want to go now?"

Matteo twisted around and glanced at me. "Where would Jonah be?"

She huffed out her best sixteen-year-old sigh. "Ugh, you guys are obsessed with him. I guess we can check City Hall. He spends a lot of time there. Or at least someone there will be able to reach him. Go straight. This road leads to the center of the City."

Silas eased the Turtle forward, and the rest of us were glued to the windows, trying to take everything in. There wasn't much on the outskirts of town; mostly parks and small clusters of bungalows. I glanced behind us, shocked at how dark it was. It was a startling contrast to the blue, sunny skies above us. There didn't seem to be any walls or fences at the edge of the city, but the eyewall of Goliath created a very clear, natural boundary.

A few shops appeared on the sides of the roads. The buildings looked new and clean, but I also got the vibe of an old-timey town, with ice cream shops and bookstores. Baskets of flowers hung from every awning, and every other block there was a grassy square in the middle of the street that had benches under shady trees.

"Hey, Cyra," Luca said.

Cyra was slumped down, not as enthralled with the outside as the rest of us were. "What?"

"Where are the people?"

She glanced out the window, then sat up straight. "Uh, I don't know."

I looked past her to the vacant street. "What do they usually do this time of day?"

Cyra's eyes had filled with worry. "I mean, this street is always busy. There are always people walking around and stuff. You know, just living, I guess. But this is creepy."

"Are we still going the right way?" Silas asked.

She nodded. "Yeah. Um, maybe we could stop at my house? I just really feel like I should check on my parents."

"Where is your house?"

She leaned over the seat. "It's on the way, I promise. You'll have to make one turn, about a mile before we get to City Hall. Dad says we were lucky to get our house, because we are close enough to walk or scooter everywhere. Everyone else has to wait for the solar buses."

My heart sank. I was so close to finding Dad, and now we had another stop to make. I closed my eyes and took a slow breath in through my nose. Dad was here. He wasn't going anywhere. I could wait a few more minutes.

I opened my eyes to find Luca studying my face. My cheeks warmed, and I looked away. He grabbed my hand. "We're almost there, Booker."

I nodded and squeezed his hand. "I know."

We turned where Cyra told us to and drove down a street lined with nicer houses than we had seen on the outskirts of town. Each yard was meticulously maintained, and there were hibiscus flowers of every color everywhere.

"Whoa. It's like a garden paradise here," I said.

Cyra grunted. "Yeah. Mom thinks I should commit to the garden team. I mean, I'm good with flowers, but I don't want that to be my whole life. There, that's our house. The one with the yellow and orange flowers."

Silas stopped the Turtle, and we all got out to stretch our legs while Cyra ran inside. The sun was warm. Along with the sunlight, the warmth wasn't something we were used to after six days in the cold wind and rain of Goliath.

"This is creepy, right?" I asked Luca. "This sun, and blue sky, and warmth, and beautiful city after driving through a wasteland for the past week."

He nodded. "The Storm Chasers have been talking about this city for years, but I realized I'm not sure I ever believed them. But they were right. Which reminds me. We have to record this." He pulled out a com and started snapping pictures of Cyra's house and the street.

I pointed to the distance. "Make sure you get Goliath in there. So they don't think we're just in some random town somewhere."

Cyra burst out of her house, her eyes wild. "They're not here. Mom should be here. She always stays home on Saturdays. She calls it her 'Day of Peace.'"

We gathered in a group next to the Turtle. I put my hand on Cyra's arm. "Can you call them? Do you have coms?"

She wrinkled her nose. "Coms? You mean phones? Yeah, we have phones. And duh, I tried that. Both of their phones are still plugged into the chargers next to their bed."

Matteo folded his arms. "Do you have any other ideas about where they might be? Out with friends?"

Cyra squeezed her eyes shut. "I guess they could be doing a shelter drill. We do those sometimes. My parents told me that before I was born, the eyewall broke down or something, and a storm with a tornado passed through the east section of the City. So they make us do drills in case something breaks down with the eyewall fence."

Silas gave a nod. "Okay. So, where do you shelter for these drills?"

Cyra's eyes popped open, and she looked sheepish. "City Hall."

Matteo grinned. "See? All roads lead to City Hall, just like you said."

She sighed and gave a small smile. "Sorry, guys."

I shook my head. "Don't be sorry. I understand what it is like to want to do anything to find your parents."

Cyra turned large eyes to me. "Well, I am sorry. You must miss your dad, and I'm sorry I was such a brat about it." Her expression brightened. "Hey. If they're in a shelter drill, then that's where Jonah will be, too. Come on."

We all jumped in the Turtle, and Silas pushed toward the center of town.

Cyra switched on a chatterbox mode, a mode we hadn't seen from her before. "It's good the streets are empty. Sometimes it can take forever to get to City Hall from our house, only because there are always so many people on the streets. The walkers have the right of way, and we'd have to wait for them to move. And right there is the cafe where they all go all the time, so it always takes a long time to get through this section. Look, you can see City Hall from here. It's the tallest building in our city."

Cyra pointed, and sure enough, a massive white dome stood above the rest of the buildings. "Turn right up there, Silas. It's a straight shot from that point."

The Turtle was so long that making turns wasn't easy. But Silas eased the Turtle into a wide right turn and swore as he came to a stop.

Soldiers blocked the road. There must have been hundreds of them.

Cyra's mouth dropped open. "What is this?"

Matteo grunted. "Those, my friend, are soldiers."

"Like, from war?"

"Yes."

We sat in the Turtle and stared out the front window.

"Well? What now?" I asked.

Silas shrugged. "I guess we wait."

"Should we get out?"

"No. The Turtle is bulletproof. We are not. Let's see if someone comes to talk to us."

We only had to wait a few minutes before the soldiers in the middle of the group parted, and a woman dressed in a beachy sundress walked out between them, her long blonde hair tossed by the breeze.

"It's Adele!" Cyra said. "She's the mayor. We can talk to her."

Adele stopped between us and the soldiers, a full block away from where we had stopped. She smiled and waved.

"I guess she wants us to get out to talk to her," Silas said.

"That seems like a bad idea," Luca growled.

"She's nice. I promise. Do you want me to go?" Cyra asked.

"No," Matteo said. "We'll all go. It's not like we could get this Turtle away fast anyway, right?"

Silas sighed. "No. I'd have to back it out. Those soldiers could surround us before I got far enough to point us back down the way we came."

Matteo nodded. "Silas, Luca, keep your guns ready, but leave them hidden."

Cyra's mouth dropped open. "You guys have guns?"

"They do, but keep that quiet, okay? Please?"

She looked uncomfortable, but nodded. We all got out of the Turtle and walked in a tight group toward Adele, with Silas, Luca, and Matteo walking in front of Cyra and me.

"Hello, friends!" Adele called out. "We've been expecting you."

We looked at each other, confused.

"You've been expecting us?" Silas called back. "Is that why you brought your army?"

Adele laughed and rolled her eyes, then turned back to the soldiers and gave a little wave. They didn't move. "Sorry, I know they're overkill. They're not my army, by the way. They were sent for our protection, but I'm sure you realize we don't need protection in here. Goliath is the one who keeps us safe, and if he lets you through, then you are definitely a friend."

"Talking about Goliath as if it's alive is creepy," Luca said under his breath.

Cyra stepped out from behind Silas. "Adele! We have to talk to you!"

Adele's mouth dropped open, and the aura of control she had exuded slipped a little. "Cyra?"

She nodded. "Yeah. Those guns are making me nervous. Can they go away?"

Adele hurried up to our group and grabbed Cyra in a hug. "Where have you been? We've been worried sick! Your mom is beside herself."

Cyra twisted her mouth. "Uh, we can talk about that later. Also, where is Mom? And everyone else?"

Adele looked her over, as if looking for signs of hurt. "They're in the shelter."

"Why?"

Adele glanced at the rest of us. "It was just a precaution recommended by a friend who told us this group was coming."

Matteo spoke. "And who told you we were coming?"

Adele smoothed back Cyra's hair, then pulled her into a side hug. "Oh come on. You don't really think that we're unaware of what goes on out in Goliath, do you? Every smart civilization knows what goes on beyond its borders."

"And what have you heard about us?"

Adele peeked past Matteo at me. "Well, we heard she was coming."

My mouth dropped open, and I stepped forward. "You did?"

Adele smiled. "Yes. And there is someone here who is dying to talk to you, Ashlyn."

My stomach skyrocketed on a roller coaster ride. "Where is he?"

Adele squeezed Cyra's shoulders. "I'll take you to him, but your friends have to wait out here. I'm sorry, it's protocol.

We're glad you're here, but you *are* outsiders. I can only take Ashlyn inside."

Luca put himself between me and Adele. "No way. That's not smart."

I put my hand on Luca's arm. "Please, Luca. It'll be okay. I'll be right back out, right?"

Adele grinned. "Of course. You guys can wait right outside in the courtyard. In fact, you can see some of Cyra's beautiful creations. She worked on our courtyard, just before she went missing."

Cyra rolled her eyes, but couldn't keep the pride off of her face. "As if no one ever thought to create a canopy of flowers before."

Adele beamed. "Come on. These guys will let you pass. I'll take Ashlyn to her appointment, and then I'll grab your parents to come out to you, Cyra. All right?"

Silas narrowed his eyes. "And will we get a chance to ask some questions?"

Adele laughed, her laughter sounding musical. "Of course. But come on, I can't keep Ashlyn's appointment waiting. He's been so eager."

Luca frowned, but he nodded. Adele gave a nod of satisfaction and turned toward the soldiers. They parted to let us all through, and we walked into the courtyard of City Hall. Adele was right; it was beautiful. But I didn't want to spend any time looking. Cyra took the guys over to a grouping of benches clustered near a gurgling fountain, and I followed Adele up the steps into City Hall.

The inside of City Hall was as vacant as the rest of the town. Adele hurried past the large central desk, toward an unmarked door. "This way, please."

I practically had to run to keep up with her, but at the same time had to stop myself from running past her, since I didn't know where I was going. All I knew was that my dad was somewhere beyond that door.

Adele pushed through the door and pointed to a door on the left. "In there. Go ahead; I'll wait outside."

I froze for a minute. I hadn't even taken a chance to look in a mirror to see what I looked like. I reached for the messy buns that had been in place for days.

Adele chuckled. "You look fine."

I smiled, took a deep breath, and pushed open the door.

I stepped all the way inside, then stopped, confused. The room appeared empty, except for a chair in front of a large screen. Adele gave me a wink and pulled the door shut.

A voice came on over a hidden speaker. "Hello, Ashlyn."

My blood ran cold as the screen turned on.

Chip smiled at me.

Chapter 25

My mouth went dry, and I stood there like an idiot.

Chip chuckled. "You're so cute when you're caught off guard."

Rage filled my belly and my senses came back. "You."

He shook his head. "You're that surprised? Come on. You're smarter than that. I'm proud of you. You made it a day sooner than I thought you would."

I clenched my fists and took a step closer to the screen. "Where. Is. Dad."

Chip set his mouth. "I don't know. I'm not lying when I say I haven't seen him for ten years. Of course, I've made sure of that. I never want to lie to your mom when I say that I don't know where your dad is."

"But you know he's here."

"Do I? Like I said, I haven't seen him. Adele has always been so kind to assist me in that area. But I am glad to see you. Your mom has been worried sick. And I can't wait to be the one to tell her you're okay."

I wanted to scream, but took a deep breath. I could tell Chip was in his office at USHA Headquarters. "Why don't you just let me talk to her? I mean, she's just down the hall from you, right?"

He gave a little shrug. "Actually, she's not here right now. I sent her home the minute I got word your team had made it. She's been a good team player, getting her work done during this trying time of having her daughter missing. But I felt it was a good day for her to spend time at home with her three remaining children."

Bile rose in my throat. "How dare you? I thought you loved her."

Anger flashed in Chip's eyes. "I *do* love her. Which is why I'm going to tell her that my team received word that you and those stupid Storm Chasers made it to the eye. But then Goliath ramped back up, and my team was unable to retrieve you. It would be too dangerous for them or for you. So now we'll just have to wait for Goliath to calm back down, which, sadly, might not be for another ten years."

I felt the blood leave my head, and my stomach rolled as I clutched the back of the chair and tried not to fall over. I had walked into a trap. And now I was stuck.

"Oh, good girl," Chip said. "You're getting it. I'm so sorry it had to be this way, but I could tell from that little chat that we had last month that the only way my plans were going to work was if you were out of the way. And I'm not a monster. I wasn't going to have you killed or anything else you seem to have conjured up in your head that I might do. But the eye of the Goliath is the safest place for you. So I made sure you got there okay."

The audacity. "Oh really? You made sure I got here okay?"

Chip grinned. "Of course. I told you, I am the hurricane keeper. You think your journey was safe by accident?"

"Safe? Like when we almost got sucked off the road three times by tornados? Or like when our second Turtle *did* get blown off the road? Are you going to tell Mom about that?"

Chip's face clouded over. "That wasn't my doing. I told them not to do it. I'll deal with them accordingly."

I glanced back at the door. "Well, thanks for the chat. I'm sure I'll see you again soon. We got into the eye, we'll get back out. And when we do, we'll have all the evidence we need to show the world what you've done here. So hold off on spending on that farce of a presidential campaign. You might need those funds for your lawyer when you go to trial for crimes against the United States."

Chip laughed. "Oh, Ash. You are so spunky and I love it. But here's the thing. You aren't leaving. If you check whatever tech pad you stole from USHA, you'll realize that Goliath is already back at the top of a category five hurricane. In fact, it's going to move up to a category six here by next week. I can't wait to introduce the world to a category six. I think they're going to name the new categorization scale 'the Sinclair Scale.' Has a nice ring to it, doesn't it?"

I stared at the screen. "You're bluffing."

"No, sweetheart. I'm not. And here's the thing. If you are a good girl and do your best to become a contributing member of that society, I'll let you see your family in a few years. Maybe right before the presidential election. Ooo, that's a great idea. It'll be the October surprise that always pops up before an election that tips the scales in favor of one candidate. I'll finally work it out to show the world that I have established one video link with the eye, and I was able to reunite you with your mom and siblings. The public will eat it up."

I rolled my eyes. "And then I'll tell them what you've done."

Chip's eyes narrowed, and he leaned in so that his entire ugly face filled the screen. "No, you won't. Because you have other people you love, right? Your BFF and her family? How about your grandparents? And the weather can be so unpredictable. Clearly, you have experienced what is capable with tornados. What you don't know is that right now, we're keeping them within the boundaries of the hurricane, because it makes the most sense. But that's only because we want to, not because we have to. Understand?"

A rock grew in my throat. I backed away. I had to get out of there.

"Leaving?" Chip asked. "Okay, but tell Chapman his check is in the mail!"

I pulled open the door and ran out, slamming the door behind me.

Adele stood at the end of the hall. She gave a small smile. "Are you set?"

I stopped. "You're working with *him*?"

She shrugged. "Someday you'll understand. He has done wonderful things for this community. And he asks for very little in return."

"Except kidnapping, apparently."

Her confident look slipped a little, then she put it back in place. "My understanding is that you came down here on your own. That's not kidnapping. And now Goliath is too dangerous to navigate. Sometimes we have to live with the consequences of our actions."

I couldn't even deal with her anymore. I pushed past her and ran through the empty building out to the courtyard. Luca, Matteo, and Silas were still sitting by the fountain. As soon as I saw Luca, I lost it. I ran to him, sobbing.

He pulled me into a hug and rubbed my hair. "Hey. What happened? Where's your dad?"

I shook my head and tried to calm down. "He wasn't in there. Chip was."

Silas stood up. "Chip was in there?"

I wiped my cheeks. "I mean, he was on a video chat. He's taking credit for us getting here safely. And he said that he has already pumped up the power on Goliath so we can't get out. It'll be a Category six by next week."

Matteo shook his head. "That's not possible."

Another sob choked out. "He said that I'm trapped here, and he's going to be the one to tell Mom that he got word that I'm safe. But that I'm stuck, and will be for ten more years."

Luca pushed me back a little so he could look me in the eyes. "We're going to figure this out. Okay?"

I sank down to the bench. "How? Adele is working with him. She said she was. She said that Chip helps this community, so they're willing to do what he asks."

Silas sat next to me and put his head in his hands. "I can't believe it. I mean, I should have seen this."

I sniffed. "Should have seen what?"

"Seen USHA's influence over this. The fact that we never saw any of the convoy on the road. The fact that the wind had died down just enough for us to get through. I should have known this was a trap."

Chip's last words replayed in my head, and I stood up and backed away from Silas. "Wait, how do I know you weren't a part of this?"

Silas looked up, confusion written all over his face. "What?"

"Chip said to tell Chapman that his check was in the mail. That's you, right? Silas Chapman? What is Chip sending you? What did you get for bringing me here?"

Luca's face darkened as he looked back and forth between me and Silas. He took a step toward me. "Yeah, Silas. What did you get out of this? Did you get a bonus for having my dad killed?"

Silas jumped up and put his hands in the air. "What are you talking about? Ashlyn, Chip is just trying to get in your head. I was just following the data that the Storm Chasers had put together. Luca, you know this. You, me, and your dad planned this whole thing together."

Luca stood frozen. I glanced around the courtyard, the flowers dancing on the balmy breeze. It was amazing how quickly a beautiful paradise could turn into a prison. I had always wanted to see some place warm and tropical. But now I desperately wanted to get back to the mountains and the cold, brown Colorado spring.

Another sob caught in my throat. "Well, now we're stuck here. For ten years."

Luca shook out of his trance and grabbed my hand. "So, where's your dad?"

I shrugged. "I guess he's here somewhere. Chip didn't deny it. He just said he hasn't seen him in ten years, and he's made sure to keep it that way, so he didn't have to lie to my mom about that." My stomach rolled again, and this time I thought I might throw up. Chip had orchestrated this whole thing flawlessly. He tied up loose ends, and he was going to get away with everything.

Cyra came over to me and put her arm around me. "He is here. I promise. We just have to find him. As soon as my parents come out of the shelter, we'll ask. Trust me, he is never far from my parents, no matter how many times I've told him he should find new friends. In fact, now that you're here, maybe he'll leave us alone."

"What are you doing here?" A man with longish brown hair and a beard rushed into the courtyard and made a beeline for Cyra. He grabbed her by the shoulders and pulled her away from our group, putting himself between us and her. "I told you to get out of here and never come back. Why didn't you listen to me?"

Cyra's eyes were wide, and she put her hands up to cover her face from the sudden attack.

"Hey!" Matteo grabbed the guy and pulled him off of Cyra. "Don't touch her!"

The man pushed back, and they fell to the ground in a scuffle. Silas and Luca jumped into the mix, pulling apart the two. Matteo got to his feet, his hands clenched and his face red.

"Back off," Matteo said between clenched teeth.

The man stood up, his back to the rest of us. He paused and looked at Matteo up and down, as if sizing him up. A primal growl rumbled out of the man's chest. "You."

Matteo's eyes got wide about a second before the man pulled his fist back and punched Matteo square in the nose. Matteo clutched his face and stumbled back, blood pouring out of his fingers.

This time, we all sprang to action. Silas and Luca jumped on the man and pinned him to the ground, while Cyra and I ran to Matteo. Matteo waved us back and looked at me with sorrow in his eyes. "I'm sorry," he garbled out.

I was so confused. "Sorry?"

Luca and Silas had the man on the ground, with Silas behind him wrapped in a wrestling bear hug, and Luca holding down his legs. The man fought and grunted for a few more seconds before realizing he wasn't going anywhere.

I stepped over to the man and got a good look at his face. My mouth dropped open and tears filled my eyes. "Dad?"

The man stopped struggling and looked at me. Confusion danced across his face for a minute, then all the blood drained out and his cheeks turned white. "Mella?"

I laughed a little and shook my head. "It's me. Ashlyn."

He gasped. "Ashlyn? Oh, honey. Why did you come?"

Acknowledgements

The love, encouragement, and support I receive is what keeps me going.

Especially thank you to Dad, Megan, Mindy, Lori, Kara, Kristen, Krystal, and Maria for their valuable insight and input.

If I had to build a hurricane shelter, I'd make sure there was room in it for all of you.

About the Author

Victoria lives at the foot of the Rocky Mountains in Colorado with her husband, her three girls, and her unemployed housecat. She is a a full-fledged homebody, a so-so housekeeper, a mediocre musician, an amateur weather nerd, and has dreamed of writing her whole life.

Also by Victoria Kimble

YA Thrillers
The Hurricane Trilogy
The Hurricane Keeper

Contemporary YA Fiction
The Main Dish

Faith- Based Middle Grade Contemporary Fiction
The Choir Girls Series
Soprano Trouble
Alto Secrets
Harmony Blues
Solo Disaster

Writing Prompts for Humans
Writing Prompts for the Hungry
Writing Prompts for the Animal Lover
Writing Prompts for the Nerds, Geeks, & Dorks
Writing Prompts for the Outdoorsy
Writing Prompts for the Suspicious